DANIEL COLTON
UNDER FIRE

This Book was placed in the Church Library by

John & Prissy White
in honor of
Roy White

A COLTON COUSINS ADVENTURE

DANIEL COLTON UNDER FIRE

ELAINE SCHULTE

Zondervan Publishing House
Grand Rapids, Michigan

A Division of HarperCollins*Publishers*

Lake Shore Baptist Church

Daniel Colton Under Fire
Copyright © 1992 by Elaine Schulte

Requests for information should be addressed to:
Zondervan Publishing House
Grand Rapids, Michigan 49530

Library of Congress Cataloging-in-Publication Data

Schulte, Elaine L.
    Daniel Colton under fire / Elaine L. Schulte
       p. cm. — (A Colton cousins adventure : bk. 2)
    Summary: On the Oregon Trail with his family in 1848, twelve-year-old Daniel tries to become a true frontiersman while dangerous Indians, a buffalo stampede, and other hardships make him glad to have God on his side.
    ISBN 0-310-54821-7 (paper)
    [1. Oregon Trail—Fiction. 2. Overland journeys to the Pacific—Fiction. 3. Frontier and pioneer life—Fiction. 4. Christian life—Fiction.] I. Title. II. Series: Schulte, Elaine L. Colton cousins adventure : bk. 2.
PZ7.S3867Dan   1992
[Fic]—dc20   91-36556
                                                  CIP
                                                   AC

All characters are fictitious with the exception of the famous trapper, Jedediah Smith.

Edited by Anne Severance
Interior designed by Louise Bauer
Cover designed by Jack Foster
Illustrations by Dan Johnson

Printed in the United States of America

92 93 94 95 96 / AM / 10 9 8 7 6 5 4 3 2 1

To the Shining Lights
on Greenfield Drive in El Cajon

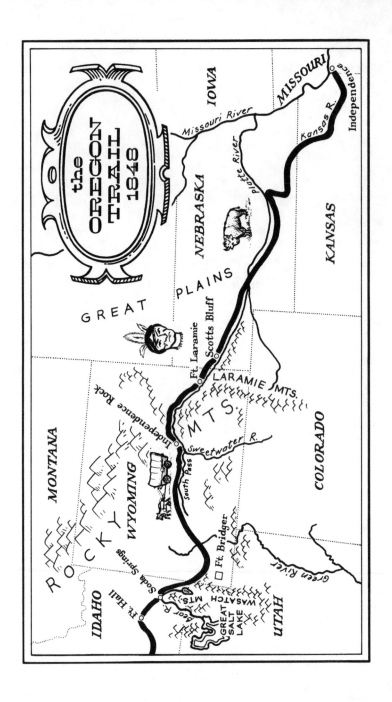

the OREGON TRAIL 1848

CHAPTER ONE

Get up ... get up, Daniel! We're leaving today!"

Daniel Colton blinked his eyes open once, then again, and quickly came awake. It took only a second or two to recognize his surroundings. He was in the covered wagon in the back yard of Aunt Pearl's log home in Independence, where he'd slept all week for what he called "frontiering practice."

"Daniel Meriwether Colton!" called his cousin, Suzannah, loud enough to wake up everyone in the state of Missouri. "Are you planning to stay in bed all day? It's the third of May, in the year 1848—the day we leave for the Oregon Territory!"

Daniel felt the shudder of the wagon as Suzannah bounced up the tongue, and he scrambled out of his bedroll. "Coming ... I'm coming—"

"Thought I'd have to pour a dipper of cold water down your neck!" she exclaimed. "Are you dressed?"

He was relieved to see he wasn't in his long underwear, but still wore his new shirt and brown homespun trousers from the day before. "Must have fallen asleep with my clothes on," he confessed sheepishly.

Twelve-year-old Suzannah pushed aside the white canvas flap by the driver's seat and poked her head in. Her brown hair was freshly braided and she was already dressed in a new red calico frock in honor of the day.

Her blue-green eyes sparkled with mischief. "Thought you'd sleep right through and miss the whole journey!"

"Ha! No chance of that, with all the racket around here!" Outside, a cow bawled and chickens squawked as they were caged for the trip.

Despite his enthusiastic greeting, Daniel couldn't help

the cold knot of fear that lodged in the pit of his stomach at the thought of the coming journey. Hurriedly, he pulled on his new cowhide boots.

Suzannah eyed the insides of the wagon. "It sure is crowded in here."

"You're right about that." He jammed his bedroll in above the barrels of rice, beans, flour, and cornmeal they had packed only yesterday. "We were told to prepare for at least six months, remember? It's a long way to Oregon."

Daniel had also made sure that his favorite books— two novels by James Fenimore Cooper—were packed in his knapsack. When the chores were done at home, he'd often lost himself for hours at a time reading the adventures of Leatherstocking. Along with David and Joshua in the Bible, Leatherstocking was his hero—brave and strong, honest and true.

After a moment, he added, "Guess I'm glad everything went wrong here in Independence . . . or maybe I should say *right*."

Suzannah turned and balanced her way back down the wagon tongue. "You're not the only one."

Daniel followed, holding out his arms as he teetered on the wooden beam, thinking of the events that had brought them here to the edge of the wilderness.

First, Aunt Pearl, who'd invited them to move here from the East, had married a widower with a half-grown son. She'd written to tell them about her marriage and their plans to move out West, but the letter hadn't arrived before his family had left Georgetown. Because she had bided her time until her new husband and his son returned from visiting relatives in St. Louis, her news had exploded like Fourth of July fireworks.

Second, Father had planned to start a frontier trading post in Independence, but before their arrival, the agent sold their three Conestoga wagons and goods by mistake.

As if that weren't enough trouble, with all the emigrants moving West, there were no houses left to buy in or around Independence.

Last week Mother had said, "It looks as if the good Lord has closed the door to our staying here." Then she had given Father a shy smile. "But I had a dream recently."

"A dream?"

She nodded. "We were riding across the prairie in a covered wagon. The sky was a great blue bowl overhead. Wildflowers bloomed all around us in the grasses and, when I woke up, I thought, 'Why, I do believe we're to go with Pearl to the Oregon Territory.'"

Father had grinned the famous Colton grin. "I've never said much about it, Ruthie girl, but it's always been in my heart to go to Oregon."

Right now, in the back yard of Aunt Pearl's log cabin, three large covered wagons stood ready, their gleaming white tops stretched tight over wooden frames to protect all the goods needed to set up new homes, farms, and businesses on the frontier. The lead wagon belonged to Aunt Pearl, Uncle Karl, and his son Garth. Father would drive the second, where Daniel and his mother would ride. The third would carry Suzannah and her family—her older sister Pauline, Pauline's husband Charles, and their little son Jamie.

As they neared the house, Daniel thought of Suzannah. Since her parents were dead and she was living with her sister, she really didn't have much choice about making the journey. She had nowhere else to go.

"Sure you don't mind going?" he asked her.

Suzannah shook her head, her braids bobbing against her shoulders. "I can't wait! Besides—" she eyed the modest cabin—"this town is too . . . ramshackle."

"That's the word, all right—ramshackle," he agreed.

When they'd arrived about two weeks ago, Independence had appeared to be a frontier town on the move. Signs reading "Goods for Oregon and California! Goods for Santa Fe!" were posted in many storefronts, and the dirt streets bustled with buggies, drays, oxcarts, and covered wagons. On the wooden sidewalks were traders, trappers, Indians, and bullwhackers.

"I'd always thought Independence, Missouri, would be the best town in the West," Daniel said. "But when we got here, I saw it was only shanties and lean-tos put up by folks on their way to more exciting places."

"Like us," Suzannah said.

"Yep, like us. But we don't know much about westering," Daniel admitted, "except what we learned at the emigration meetings."

"Why, Daniel Meriwether Colton, we're nearly *all* greenhorns at covered wagon travel," she replied as they hurried up the path. "Besides, Meriwethers are supposed to have itchy, adventurous feet, aren't they?"

It was true. Daniel had been excited by reports of the frontier for as long as he could remember. He and his father were even middle-named "Meriwether" for Captain Meriwether Lewis, who had explored the Oregon Territory and was a friend of the family. As a boy, Father had heard about the great expedition from Captain Lewis himself.

Suddenly Daniel grinned. "Would you like to hear what I heard about Oregon in town?"

"Maybe so and maybe not," she teased. When he made a move to pull one of her thick braids, she jerked out of reach. "Stop it! Now tell me."

"Father and I had just passed the bank when a man hauled a box out onto the sidewalk, stood up on it, and began to talk about Oregon. He said that out there the pigs run about under great acorn trees, round and fat and already cooked. What's more, the pigs have forks and knives sticking in them so you can cut off a slice whenever you're hungry."

"You don't expect me to believe that!"

"Never know what you'll believe!" He laughed, then had to duck away from her balled fist.

At the house, they scraped the mud from their boots, while Aunt Pearl's two collie dogs—Lad and Lass—ran out from around back, barking in welcome.

Daniel leaned over to rub their necks. "Even *you* know something's about to change, don't you?"

"Don't let them in," Suzannah warned as she opened the back door. "Uncle Karl will have us skinned."

Daniel gave the dogs a last fond pat. "Stay, boy. Stay, girl," he said, and hurried in behind Suzannah.

Even the back hall of the log house smelled of bacon, flapjacks, and freshly baked bread. His mother, lending a hand in Aunt Pearl's kitchen, seemed right at home.

"Good morning, Daniel," she greeted him, her round face wreathed in a cheery smile. She wore a huge white apron over a new blue calico frock, making her look a bit plumper. Father called her "Ruthie Sunshine," which suited her. "Thought you'd decided to stay here, after all," she teased, pulling a loaf of bread from the oven.

"Not me!"

Aunt Pearl was piling flapjacks on a huge platter. It still surprised Daniel how much she looked like Mother, with her blond hair pulled back in a knot at the back of her head, only Aunt Pearl was younger and slimmer. "I suggested we pack the quilts and churn on top of you in the wagon, but your mother talked me out of it," his aunt said.

Mother laughed. "He'd have been sure to crack his head on the iron skillet or something else when we got moving." She told Daniel, "Wash up, then get to the table and eat a hearty breakfast. We made a big one to start out on, since cooking won't be as easy on the way."

He headed back to the hallway table, where the pitcher of water and basin were kept. Studying his reflection in the mirror, he saw just what he expected to see—a freckle-faced, almost thirteen-year-old boy with green eyes and wavy brown hair topped by a stubborn cowlick. Mother often said he was the very image of his father, but he wasn't too sure of it.

He wiped his hands on the snowy towel his aunt had laid out for him. Then, giving his cowlick a final swipe, he hurried to join the others at the long plank table.

"Morning," he said, climbing over the bench and sitting between Suzannah and Father. "Sorry I overslept."

"Guess you must have been tuckered out." His father's grin didn't stop at the corners of his mouth, but spread all the way up to his crinkly eyes.

"I nearly shook the wagon to bits before he finally woke up," Suzannah informed them.

Father chuckled at her remark, but Uncle Karl saw no humor in it. Uncle Karl was a tall, bony man with skin as brown as an Indian's and an Adam's apple that bobbed when he swallowed. This morning he wore old buckskins and a frown that pulled his dark bushy brows together.

"Ain't no sleepin' late on the trail, boy."

"Yes, sir."

Like the rest of his family, Daniel couldn't understand why Aunt Pearl had married such a stern man as Karl Stengler. Father guessed it was from loneliness after her husband and two children had died last summer of ague and fevers. But Mother had said, "I do believe sorrow caused poor Pearl to lose her head."

Across the table, his new fourteen-year-old step-cousin, Garth, glowered from beneath dark brows exactly like Uncle Karl's. "See you made it through the night again out in the wilds of our back yard," he mumbled through a mouth full of flapjack.

Daniel managed a smile. "Yep. I made it."

"So no big bad wolf gobbled up the city boy?"

"Not yet," Daniel replied good-naturedly. He hoped that not arguing with his stepcousin would put an end to the remarks, but it didn't.

"Don't see what good it does to sleep out, anyhow," the boy continued. "Ain't likely to run into any savage Injuns or wild animals there."

"Just practicing," Daniel explained. Maybe Garth was right, but sleeping out in the wagon sure beat being under the same roof as his grouchy stepcousin.

"You sure do *need* the practice, never mind your high 'n' mighty airs about knowin' Meriwether Lewis."

Daniel decided to ignore Garth and filled his own plate with eggs and flapjacks.

Aunt Pearl patted his shoulder as she poured him a glass of milk from the pitcher, then stepped around the table to pour another glass for her stepson. "I'm glad to see you enjoying my cooking at last, young man. "

"Humph! Ain't near as good as my real ma's," muttered Garth without looking up.

"No call to complain, boy," said Uncle Karl. "Your stepma's doin' her best."

Daniel was pleased to see that his aunt's disposition was a lot like Mother's. His aunt simply put a hand on her hip, smiled sweetly, and said, "Garth Stengler, I'm going to win you over yet, you just wait and see."

Uncle Karl grinned, but Garth just kept on eating.

Daniel was tempted to say that the flapjacks looked like the best he'd ever eaten. Instead, he asked, "Where are Pauline, Charles, and Jamie?"

"Pauline said they'd be here in a minute." Father paused, a forkful of eggs on the way to his mouth. "It takes a while to get a little one dressed."

Daniel spread butter over his steaming flapjacks and

watched it soak in. He had heard Charles ride in late last night, but he decided not to mention it. Come to think of it, he wasn't sure now if Pauline's husband had been riding in . . . or out.

"We've already said grace," Father told him.

Daniel ducked his head for a quick prayer of his own. There'd be plenty to do, he reflected as he began to eat— more provisions to pack, oxen to yoke and chain together, milk cow and other livestock to round up—

A few minutes later, Cousin Pauline arrived, little Jamie toddling by her side. Her golden hair gleamed in the sunlight, but her eyes were red from crying and her beautiful face was pale with strain.

She handed Father a letter. "You may as well read it aloud so everyone knows."

Trouble, Daniel thought. *More trouble with Charles. He's probably been gambling again.*

Father glanced down at the letter in dismay, then read:

> Dear Pauline,
>
> By the time you read this, I'll be on my way elsewhere. I will not return to Virginia, so you can probably guess where I am going. Nonetheless, I will not tell you so that, if you are questioned, you can truthfully say you don't know.
>
> I enclose sufficient funds for your needs. I expect to catch up with you somewhere along the way.
>
> Your husband,
> Charles

Suzannah gasped, and Daniel understood how she felt. She'd given up all the gold coins her father had left her to pay for Charles's gambling debts back home in Virginia.

Why, she had saved her brother-in-law's life! Now it appeared he was up to his old tricks.

Daniel whispered to her, "Guess we shouldn't be too surprised. It's the same thing he did all the way from Virginia—gambled in a town until he got in trouble, then moved on ahead of us down the National Road."

She let out an angry breath. "He must have cheated at gambling. Let's hope no one's after him *again.*"

At the head of the table, Uncle Karl leaned back in his chair. "Charles Herrington might be pleasin' to look at, but he don't strike me as none too reliable."

Tears welled in Pauline's eyes, and she turned to lift Jamie into the highchair. "He may not be perfect," she replied in a choked voice, "but he's my husband."

"Then I'd say you ain't much of a judge, missy," said Uncle Karl bluntly.

It was all Daniel could do to keep quiet. Finally he squared his shoulders and spoke up. "Did you have to make Pauline feel worse than she already does?"

The next moment he knew he had made a mistake, for his father gave him a warning look.

A long silence filled the log room, and Daniel wondered if Aunt Pearl might apologize to Pauline for her new husband's rude comment. But when he darted a glance at his aunt, he saw that she had pressed her lips together as if she were guarding her tongue.

At that moment little Jamie grabbed a spoon and pounded the tray of his wooden highchair. "Eat!" he cried. "Eat!"

The laughter that followed relieved the tension, and everyone finished their breakfast with light-hearted conversation.

At last Father pushed back his plate and heaved a deep sigh. "Ladies, you have outdone yourselves. Now, I'd best be helping Karl with the chores, or we won't be leaving today, after all." He rose, towering above the table. "Son," he said to Daniel. "I guess you'll have to drive the wagon for Pauline, Suzannah, and Jamie."

"Me?" Daniel gulped. "I've never driven *oxen*—"

"Someone has to replace Charles," Father said.

Trying not to think of the dangers ahead, Daniel nodded. "It can't be much worse than stopping a runaway Conestoga wagon." He remembered that fearsome adventure on the way to Independence all too well.

"You'll get the hang of it." His father clapped him on the shoulder and gave him a look of confidence.

We'll find out soon enough, Daniel thought.

Across the table, Garth let out a low whistle. "I can just see it now—him sinkin' the wagon in quicksand up to its axles, or spillin' oxen and all over some cliff!"

Daniel held his temper. *I'll show him!* he thought. *If it's the last thing I do, I'll show all of them that I can be a frontiersman!*

CHAPTER
TWO

Outside the day was cloudless and bright. A balmy spring breeze played in the tops of trees in Aunt Pearl's backyard as the travelers checked off last-minute items for the journey ahead. Somewhere in the fields, a meadowlark warbled a welcome to the new day.

Everything seemed peaceful enough, at least on the surface. But Daniel felt a shiver of apprehension as he made a final inspection of the six sturdy Durham oxen yoked in pairs to pull the wagon he would be responsible for bringing safely across the wilderness. Parading back and forth beside the line-up were Lad and Lass, barking excitedly.

Beside him, Suzannah retied the bow of her new white sunbonnet under her chin. "Appears we're ready to go."

"Almost." He cast a nervous glance at the oxen, switching their tails to rid themselves of bothersome flies. "Let's hope they don't bolt."

"You worry too much," Suzannah said. "All you have to remember is 'Giddap, Gee, Haw, and Whoa.'"

"*That* much I know." Daniel clenched the bullwhip in a sweaty palm. He had only practiced cracking the whip a few times this morning, but without the team of oxen.

"Doggies . . . doggies!" Jamie squealed with delight from inside the wagon.

"Oxen," Daniel corrected him, but Jamie only yelled louder. "Doggies! Doggies!"

Pauline smiled for the first time all morning. "Don't worry about us," she told Daniel. "Jamie's tied to a sideboard. He has just enough rope to move around a bit without jumping out of the wagon."

Daniel felt a little like jumping himself. This trip had him plenty worried. *Help me, Lord,* he prayed. *I might look like a bullwhacker, but I don't feel like one. And I'm not happy about the idea of whacking oxen and tearing their hides to shreds.*

He glanced skyward, wishing God would boom out, "FEAR NOT, DANIEL." But there was only the blue sky and the shimmering sunshine. Besides, he knew God was everywhere, even in his soul, so there wasn't much sense in looking upward. The thing to do was to trust his heavenly Father.

He adjusted his broad-rimmed hat uneasily. "It would have been easier to do odd jobs like I was supposed to before Charles left and stuck me with his bullwhacking job," he muttered.

"I think it's exciting!" Suzannah replied. She lowered her voice so Pauline wouldn't hear. "Besides, do you really think Charles would have agreed to bullwhacking?"

"Probably would have been beneath him," Daniel decided. "Maybe that's why he rode on ahead."

She shrugged. "I really think he's gone off to gamble again." After a moment, she added, "Let's not talk about Charles anymore. Anyhow, today's just a practice run to the jumping-off place. We don't have to join up with the other wagons at any special time."

"What's holding us up?"

"I'll go see." Suzannah headed behind the wagon where the livestock milled about, blending their moos and bleats in a barnyard chorus.

Daniel turned a doubtful eye on the oxen, hoping the wagon wasn't too heavy for them to pull clear to Oregon. Besides baggage, they carried tools and garden implements, lanterns, canvas tents, a clever fold-out table and stools for eating, ropes and harnesses, and goods to trade with the Indians. And, of course, for the many meals they must prepare on the long journey, they had packed in more barrels, sacks, and boxes with provisions: sugar, coffee, tea, lard, baking powder, dried fruit, sides of bacon, sacks of dried peas and beans, smoked beef, and two hundred pounds of flour per person. The men would hunt for game to provide fresh meat along the way—which brought up another concern.

Daniel would have to hunt with the new flintlock rifle Father had given him—something else he'd never done at home in the city. Worse, he felt nervous around guns, maybe because of the neighbor boy back in Georgetown who'd accidentally shot his own father.

Suzannah came around from behind the wagon. "Looks like Ned Taylor is having trouble rounding up the livestock," she said of the fifteen-year-old farm boy they'd hired to tend the animals along the way. "Uncle Karl is giving him a hand."

"The animals know something's up," Daniel said. "And Ned's probably a little anxious, too. Animals can smell fear, you know." He remembered reading that somewhere in a book, and now the thought was anything but comforting.

Women's voices came from the cabin. Aunt Pearl's friends had come to bid her farewell and now helped her carry out the last of her special treasures—a small, cane-backed rocker and a blue glass lamp that her husband had given her just before he had taken sick.

Daniel shook his head. "That lamp won't make it."

Aunt Pearl's friends cried as she climbed into the first wagon, holding the lamp carefully wrapped in a quilt. "We may never see you again!"

The scene reminded Daniel of leaving his own home in Georgetown, and the tears his mother and her friends had shed at their parting. No friends, he noticed, had come to see Garth and Uncle Karl off.

When Aunt Pearl was settled, Uncle Karl rode forward on his gray stallion. "Wagons, ho!" he shouted.

"Good-bye! Good-bye, Pearl!" her friends called.

Garth raised his bullwhip and snaked it out into the air with a resounding crack. "Giddap, boys! Giddap!"

Slowly the first team of oxen began to move past the log house, then down the tree-lined path toward the main road.

"Giddap!" Father shouted and cracked his whip over the heads of the second team. The wagon moved on without difficulty, and then it was Daniel's turn.

Doing his best to imitate Garth and Father, Daniel lifted the bullwhip and gave a sharp snap of his wrist. The whip unfurled high above the oxen's backs. At the same time, he dropped his voice to its lowest pitch. "Giddap, boys, giddap!"

For an instant nothing happened. Then their massive shoulders fell against the yokes, and the great iron-rimmed wheels rolled forward. Daniel drew a sigh of relief as the wagon creaked and bumped along, following the others.

There was a kind of power about cracking the whip, he thought in surprise. A power that set things in motion.

But Uncle Karl was frowning as he rode back down the line. "Don't let up on them oxen!" he yelled to Daniel. "Let 'em know who's in charge right from the start!"

"Yes sir, I'll try!" Daniel called back.

Suzannah fell into step with him. "Does that mean you have to crack the bullwhip all the way to Oregon?"

"I'm not planning on it."

Fortunately, the path was slightly downhill, and his team plodded on behind Father's wagon without further coaxing. As they moved along, the barnyard chorale continued: the mooing of the milk cow, the lowing of the spare oxen, the cackles and crows of the chickens and roosters, and the whinnying of horses, punctuated by the sharp barks of the two collie dogs.

"Doggies!" Jamie squealed above the ruckus.

"Oregon Territory, here we come!" Suzannah yelled.

"Giddup, boys!" Daniel called out again. He felt the excitement of the high adventure ahead as well as the pang of fear that never quite disappeared.

Pauline peered out the front of the wagon with Jamie. "A good thing the wagon train hired a guide and Ned."

"Uncle Karl wasn't for it," Suzannah said. "It was your father who paid for all of our family's share."

"I'm not surprised," Daniel said, being careful not to scuff the toes of his new cowhide boots in the dust.

There was a moment of silence while they walked along the pathway beside the wagon, thinking their own private thoughts.

"Uncle Karl is a tight-fisted man in more ways than one," Suzannah said.

"What do you mean?"

"Just look how he's dressed in that greasy old buckskin."

"By the end of this journey, we may all look like that," Daniel said, "except for you, of course, with your prissy white sunbonnet."

"It's a nuisance," she complained. "Can't even see out the sides." She turned her head back and forth to show him. "But wouldn't *you* look fetching in a sunbonnet?" she said and made a swipe at his hat.

He dodged her just in time. "Hey, look out! I've got to lead these oxen."

"Then lead on!"

When they came to the main road, he yelled, "Gee! Gee!" To his relief, the oxen turned right, following the others down the dirt road that led west.

"See," Suzannah said, "it's easy." After a while she suggested, "Let's name the oxen. They're such homely old things we could give them beautiful names like . . . like flowers."

"Oxen are all 'he's'," Daniel objected. "You can't name them after *flowers!*"

"Just see if I can't!" Suzannah retorted. "Starting from the front on the left-hand side, we could call them Daisy and Petunia and Iris—"

"They all look alike to me," Daniel said. "Right now, I'm just glad they're following Father's wagon."

"Maybe they won't look alike as the days go by," Suzannah argued. "On this side, we have Marigold . . . then there's Lily and Rose."

The sun had risen higher, its warmth chasing the morning chill. All in all it was most pleasant, just walking along with Suzannah beside the oxen. As they passed through the countryside, farm children waved at them.

"Where you headed?" asked one boy.

"Going fishing!" Daniel called.

There was a ripple of laughter. "Ain't that a good

one! Goin' fishin' in Californy or the Oregon Territory, I'll warrant!"

When Father took out his harmonica and began to play "Old Dan Tucker," the bouncy tune floated out through the cool morning air, and Daniel and Suzannah sang out with the others:

> *Old Dan Tucker was a mighty man,*
> *Washed his face in a frying pan,*
> *Combed his head with a wagon wheel,*
> *Died with a toothache in his heel.*

Rich milk from Elsa, their milk cow, sloshed in the butter churn that hung beneath the wagon along with the grease bucket and the chicken coop. The hens clucked and cackled as they lurched about.

"Worst complainers on the trip so far," said Daniel.

Suzannah nodded. "Aunt Pearl's worried that they'll stop laying eggs."

"Can't say I'd blame them if they did."

The scenery became even more colorful as the freshly painted wagons rolled through green meadows abloom with wildflowers and past thick groves of oak and hickory trees. Once, Suzannah pointed out a cloud of butterflies fluttering from a field, much like the petals of flowers blown about by the wind. Birds chirped from the treetops, as if wishing them Godspeed. Every living creature seemed to be cheering them on their way, Daniel thought.

Before long, they stopped for drinks from the barrels of water lashed to the sides of the wagons. From inside, Pauline handed out their tin cups, while Mother and Aunt Pearl served flaky apple tarts baked only that morning. "To hold us till we get to the jumping-off place," they said.

"You're doing fine, son," said Father, nodding his approval.

"Well, so far, so good." Daniel took another bite of his apple tart. "Maybe driving the wagon won't be as hard as I thought."

In no time at all, Uncle Karl was rounding them up again. "Don't want that livestock to wander. Wagons, ho!"

After traveling for what seemed like hours, they spotted the "jumping-off place"—a meadow with rocky outcroppings. The meadow was dotted with the tents and camps of emigrants whose wagon trains would make up here and leave at intervals over the next few days. Beyond, lush green valleys lay between the wooded ridges.

Soon they could see the wagons already assembled for Captain Monroe's train as well as others that would be setting out before them. Lined up for as far as they could see were the white-topped wagons, their sail-like canvases billowing in the light breeze. Masses of fluffy white clouds floated lazily in the blue sky, while the great ball of the sun beamed over the landscape. Here and there, some of the women were already getting out their cooking pots for the midday meal.

Daniel was glad to see Pauline sketching the scene, as she'd often done on the trip down the National Road.

"We're almost there," he said to Suzannah. His team slowed behind Father's wagon. Then, to his amazement, Marigold, the lead ox, stopped and sat down in the middle of the trail. "Up! Get up!" he yelled.

The other oxen, thinking Daniel had said "Giddup!" tried to move on, dragging Marigold in the dirt. "Whoa! Whoa!" he shouted, and they halted in a cloud of dust. He grabbed Marigold's wooden yoke and tried to pull her up. But she refused to budge. Behind him, he could already hear the laughter of onlookers, enjoying his dilemma. Daniel felt his face grow hot.

Just then, Uncle Karl rode up on Gray. "You got to hit 'im with the bullwhip, boy. Whip 'im and cuss 'im."

Daniel swallowed hard. Never in his life had he whipped an animal, nor did he care to take up cussing. On top of that, a crowd of emigrants was gathering to watch him. Spying the small branch Suzannah had trailed along in the dirt, he suddenly had an idea.

"Whip that ox! Don't let 'im git away with it!" Uncle Karl yelled, growing red in the face.

Instead, Daniel grabbed Suzannah's branch. With the leafy side up, he tickled Marigold under the chin, then grabbed the animal's ear and yelled into it, "Come on, Marigold, stand up!"

"Marigold?" Garth repeated, loud enough for everyone to hear. "With a name like that, it's no wonder he won't git up!"

Everyone burst into laughter, but to their amazement, Marigold lumbered to his feet.

"Hey, look at that!" one emigrant exclaimed.

"Now there's a fellow who knows his oxen," said another. "Yelling in an ox's ear is better than beatin' its hide any day, I'd say!"

Daniel merely grinned. "Giddap!" he called to the team again.

The oxen moved forward and, finally, the wagon was in place in a half-circle, leaving space for more wagons.

"Watch that livestock!" Uncle Karl warned, for as soon as they were unhitched, the oxen, milk cow, and horses headed for the nearby creek to lap up the water.

After a while Garth and Uncle Karl pulled their horses, Blackie and Gray, away from the creek. "At least the oxen have more sense than horses," Uncle Karl said. "They know when to quit drinkin' so they don't git the flounders. Last thing we need is sick horses."

But Father had trouble with his new chestnut gelding, Chewning, who didn't know when he had had enough. Finally, he mounted Chewning bareback and rode him away from the creek. "It appears we have our work cut out for us," he said.

"What next?" Daniel muttered. "What next?"

Ned Taylor helped Daniel drive the oxen and milk cow back to the meadow. "The work ain't so bad," said the boy, "not if you're used to farm work like me."

Ned was thin and wiry with a mop of red curls, and his homespun shirt and trousers were as patched as a quilt. In a family of sixteen children, Daniel guessed there was never quite enough of anything to go around.

Daniel's father rode up beside them. "We'll drive picket stakes into the ground and tie the horses to them for grazing, then hobble the oxen's front legs together. Next, their hooves have to be cleaned. Later on, the wagon wheels will need greasing, and we'll be making repairs on the wagons from time to time."

"Sure is plenty to do," Daniel remarked, though he wasn't complaining.

When they had finished their chores, he strolled over to the cookfire and dropped down beside Suzannah.

"How did you ever think of tickling Marigold under the chin?" she asked.

"I saw Jamie in the wagon and you with that branch . . . and it suddenly came to me that if Jamie jumps when you tickle him under the chin, maybe the ox would, too. But I really think it was my yelling in his ear and the emigrants' roar of laughter that brought old Marigold to his feet."

"Pauline sketched the whole thing, so you'll never forget," Suzannah told him with a mischievous grin.

Daniel groaned. "Just what I always wanted!"

Nearby, Cousin Garth sat down on the ground, propped himself against a wagon wheel, and began to clean his rifle. "Well, if it ain't the famous Captain Meriwether Lewis himself—" he said, his voice dripping sarcasm—"pretendin' to be a bullwhacker."

Daniel clamped his lips shut.

"Just ignore him," Suzannah said under her breath.

But Garth wasn't through. "No one asked you to go with us!"

"Aunt Pearl did! It was her idea!" Daniel blurted.

"Her ideas don't count fer much."

Suzannah looked shocked. "She's your *mother* now."

"*Step*ma," Garth said.

Suzannah and Daniel exchanged a long look, but neither of them said anything else.

The day that had begun with the promise of fair weather was no guarantee that every other day would be sunny, Daniel realized. Right now, Garth himself looked like a dark thundercloud, ready to burst.

There was much more to crossing an unknown wilderness than the danger of attack by wild animals or Indians, Daniel decided. There was also the threat of being ridiculed and humiliated by one's fellow travelers! Daniel wasn't too sure just what he could do about it, but at the very least, he knew he had better be on the lookout for Garth Stengler!

CHAPTER
THREE

Here and there throughout the camp, cookfires flared, sending forth delicious smells as the women prepared their first meal away from home. Already, people gathered, enjoying the picnic-like atmosphere of their outing.

Nearby, a savory stew bubbled in the big cast-iron pot; its aroma mingled with that of freshly baked soda bread. Food seemed to smell better out here in the open air, Daniel thought, and he was ready to eat long before Aunt Pearl called, "Dinner!"

Daniel and Suzannah took the tin eating utensils from the grub boxes and banged the spoons against their plates. "When we finish eating, we can make music!" he joked.

Laughing, they waited in line for stew and soda bread. Suzannah had already set out the folding table and stools, and after they were served, they carried their plates to the table.

When everyone had gathered, Father took Mother's and Pauline's hands, then suggested, "Shall we thank the good Lord?"

Daniel grabbed Suzannah's hand on one side and Ned Taylor's on the other. Ned seemed surprised, as if the idea of holding hands during the family prayer were new to him, while Uncle Karl and Garth hung back in silent disapproval.

Nevertheless, Father spoke boldly. "Almighty God, our heavenly Father, we come to thank Thee for this fine spring day and this food we are about to eat. And we thank Thee most especially for Thy lovingkindness, for each of us is a sinner, saved only by Thy grace."

He paused, then added, "We know how important the family is to Thee. We ask that this family circle be strengthened, neither weakened nor broken by the trials of the long journey ahead. And we thank Thee for this fine meal prepared by loving hands. We pray in the blessed name of Thy Son, Jesus Christ. Amen."

They all dug into the hearty beef stew and buttered biscuits. Nothing had ever tasted so good! Daniel wondered if Garth would find something to complain about just to rile Aunt Pearl, but his stepcousin ate in silence.

"Let's shoot us some wild turkeys for supper," Uncle Karl said when he had taken the last bite. "How about you, Daniel? Up to some huntin'?"

Garth answered for him. "Don't count on it! He couldn't shoot a tincan off the fence post when he practiced with his new rifle at home."

"I've never hunted," Daniel admitted, feeling a wave of panic wash over him. "We . . . bought our meat at the butcher shop in Georgetown."

Garth waved his hand toward the nearby woods. "Well, this ain't Georgetown!"

"I haven't hunted for a good many years myself," Father put in quickly, "but Daniel and I will do fine in time."

Uncle Karl shook his head. "I'm countin' on it. We got plenty of food now, but if we can't shoot our dinner later, we'll all starve to death."

Starve to death? Daniel took another bite of stew, but it was hard to swallow.

"After we finish eatin', we'll set out in those trees," Uncle Karl went on. "There ought to be plenty of turkeys hereabouts."

Daniel felt Suzannah's eyes on him, and he applied himself to the food on his tin plate.

For dessert, Aunt Pearl and Mother brought out peach pies baked at home. "Enjoy them," his aunt said. "It's probably the last time you'll see a real pie till we get to Oregon. A campfire's not the best place for baking."

Garth gave her a dark look, as if to say, *My real ma could've.*

"Here, Garth," Aunt Pearl offered, "why don't you eat my piece? I'm as full as can be."

"Eat it yerself," he muttered.

Daniel glanced at his mother, who put a hand to her mouth in shock, while Uncle Karl reached over and helped himself to the pie on Aunt Pearl's plate. "Garth, you watch yourself, boy. B'lieve you owe your stepma an apology."

"Sorry," Garth mumbled, but he didn't *sound* it.

Aunt Pearl closed her eyes for an instant, then opened them and smiled at Garth. "You're forgiven," she said.

Daniel turned his attention to an incoming wagon. While they had been eating, one covered wagon after another had pulled up all around them until now they formed a large circle. Moving purposefully from group to group was a brown-bearded man Daniel had not seen before. When he asked his father, he learned it was John Monroe, the emigrant they had elected to be the captain of their wagon train. He was calling for a meeting of all heads of family in his train within the hour.

"Won't leave much time for huntin'," Uncle Karl said with disappointment.

"You and Garth go ahead," Father offered. "Daniel can help me grease the wagon wheels and check for repairs. And I'm sure Ned will keep an eye on the livestock."

"Done," Uncle Karl agreed.

Garth lost no time in fetching his rifle from the wagon, then tore off to the woods with Uncle Karl.

Father was thoughtful as he watched the two leave. "We're in no danger of starvation yet. There's leftover stew for supper, and I heard the ladies mention cornbread. We can manage without turkey tonight. Besides," he added, giving Daniel an appraising look, "you've already proved yourself this morning, Son. You've turned out to be some bullwhacker—one who uses his head instead of his whip."

Daniel drew a deep breath, wishing Garth and Uncle Karl felt the same way about him.

Later, while he sat in the wagon train meeting with the crowd of emigrants, Daniel saw Garth and Uncle Karl straggle in from the woods. "Looks like they came back empty-handed," he whispered to his father, nodding toward the returning hunters.

His father smiled, then they turned their attention to the man who would be leading their wagon train across the prairie. Captain Monroe struck Daniel as a hard man. He talked hard, worked hard, and had roamed these parts for some years as an Indian scout. His hard living was carved into his leathery face, tanned as brown as a hickory nut and about as tough. So it had come as a great surprise to Daniel that he had agreed to no liquor drinking, no gambling, and no traveling on the Sabbath, as long as they were able to cover the ground on schedule.

"Every day," Captain Monroe was saying, "the lead wagon moves to the rear of the line. We don't want the same oxen breaking trail through brambly country. Nor do we want the last wagons always traveling in the forward wagons' dust." He paused to let his instructions sink in. "Our guide is—"

"Why should we pay for a guide when we already have a captain?" one man interrupted. "We just follow the Platte River to the Snake River, then the Snake right on up to Oregon. We got maps and reports—"

Captain Monroe cut him short. "There's more to it than that." He glanced at Uncle Karl and Garth, who walked up just then with their rifles in hand. "We need someone who knows where to hunt . . . . Right here, for example, where the wagons gather, the game's all been shot off the land."

Uncle Karl and Garth looked sheepish. Before they could speak, though, the captain added, "And we need someone who knows where to cross rivers and mountains . . . and how to deal with the Indians. And that's only the beginning."

Another emigrant spoke up. "Can this guide we're payin' for get us to Oregon before the first frost?"

"No one reaches Oregon before the first frost," the captain replied, "not on a six- or seven-month trek. We'll hit frost in the mountains while it's still summer down here."

Red-faced, the man said, "Didn't think of that."

"We have a train of twenty-seven wagons—long enough to scare off trouble and short enough to keep clear of our own dust."

Nearby another emigrant nodded. "And for drawin' up quick against Indian attacks!"

"What is the situation with the Indians right now?" Father asked.

"Unless provoked, the Indians haven't been causing much trouble for wagon trains lately," Captain Monroe replied. "But keep a sharp eye on your horses. Indians think nothing of stealing horses. They figure the white man's livestock is a fair exchange for crossing their land."

Just then, Garth, who had taken a seat near Daniel, muttered hoarsely, "I'm goin' to shoot me an Indian. Maybe more 'n one."

Daniel's mouth dropped open. "You'll cause trouble for sure! You'll bring a whole war party down on us!"

Garth glared at him from under his thick, dark brows. "I reckon we'll see about that."

Traveling with Garth and his father would not be easy, Daniel thought again. Not easy at all.

When the meeting ended, Captain Monroe said, "Now go out and meet your fellow travelers. We'll be together for a long time, so let's try to be friends."

Daniel strolled around, meeting the other emigrants and their families. Besides farmers, there were saddlers who worked with leather, coopers who made barrels, a gunsmith, a minister, and even a few foreigners: a German couple, the Amptmanns and their almost-grown sons, Willie and Kurt; a French couple, the Poisots, with eight-year-old twins, Lynette and Annette. And there were the Murphys, with fifteen children spilling from their three wagons.

Suddenly four horsemen galloped into camp and reined their horses to a halt. "Where's the Colton wagons?" one of them demanded.

Daniel could already guess why they had come. This kind of thing had happened before.

"Where's Charles Herrington?" their leader asked.

"Charles isn't with us," Daniel's father replied in a

calm but firm voice. "He left Independence the night before we did."

The men looked around. "You, Karl Stengler . . . your word is good. You seen Herrington?"

Uncle Karl shook his head. "It's like Franklin Colton said. He left the night before us, no doubt fer New Orleans. Herrington's a gambler, 'n' that would suit him best. He's too lazy to put in a good day's work."

Daniel was glad Pauline wasn't within hearing distance, but Suzannah was, and her cheeks turned pink.

The men were furious. "Not only did he cheat us out of our hard-earned money, but he made fools of us right there in Independence!"

"Gambling doesn't pay," Father put in kindly.

"Never mind the sermon," the leader said. "Save it for Herrington. And if you see that card shark, tell him we won't forget!" And with that, the men wheeled their horses back toward Independence and rode away.

In a little while, Daniel saw his father talking with Pauline before wandering over to another wagon camp in the meadow. When he returned, Daniel overheard him tell Mother, "Charles rode through here early this morning with three other men on horseback. And they were in a big hurry."

Later in the evening, most of the settlers gathered around a crackling bonfire in the middle of the camp circle. Daniel learned that, after they crossed the Rocky Mountains together, ten of the wagons would break off and veer south for California, while the other seventeen would continue on to Oregon.

"Why, the sun scarcely sets in Californy, so I hear tell!" said one emigrant. "There's no ague or fever. They say it's an earthly paradise!"

"In Oregon, they've got rivers full of salmon," Uncle

Karl argued, "and there's plenty of fur to trap, and rich land that's free for the takin'."

"And, according to Daniel," said Suzannah, joining in the discussion, "acorn-fed pigs who wear knives and forks, just waiting for us to cut off a slice or two whenever we're hungry!"

The nearby emigrants laughed, and even Uncle Karl smiled.

"I'll get you for that!" Daniel promised.

She laughed. "Oh, no, you won't, Daniel Colton!"

As the sun dipped over the horizon, painting pink and purple shadows, a fiddler struck up a lively tune, and Father took out his harmonica. Soon they were singing old favorites, "On Top of Old Smoky" and "Skip to My Lou."

Between songs, Daniel saw his chance for revenge. "How about 'Oh, Suzannah' in honor of my cousin, Suzannah Elizabeth Colton?"

She elbowed him in the ribs, but he only grinned. "I said I'd get you for telling that pig story!" Then he sang out heartily with the rest of them:

Oh, I come from Alabama with my banjo on my knee,
   And I'm going to Louisiana, my true love for to see.
It rained all night the day I left;
   The weather it was dry.
The sun so hot I froze to death:
   Suzannah, don't you cry.
Oh, Suzannah, don't you cry for me;
   I've come from Alabama with my banjo on my knee.

Every time they came to the chorus, Daniel sang the name extra loud. Suzannah was a good sport about it, though, clapping with the others and bobbing her head as she sang the comical words.

The evening's entertainment ended with "hymns to

sleep on" and a prayer by the minister, James Benjamin. "Lord," he asked, "keep us safe on this journey and, more important, keep us in Thy will. In Christ's name. Amen."

Daniel and Suzannah returned to their wagons by the light of the flickering campfire and a few bright stars overhead. Other travelers camping farther down in the meadow still fiddled and sang, unwilling to end this first day on the trail.

"Come morning, we'll really be on our way," Suzannah said, yawning in spite of herself.

Daniel nodded, feeling once again the prickle of fear. In the distance, he could hear the howling of wolves. What if he couldn't do his part when their lives depended on his being able to hunt for food? What if the next time Marigold decided to balk, Daniel couldn't make him get up? And, worst of all, what if Garth had really meant what he said about killing Indians?

CHAPTER
FOUR

In his makeshift bed under the wagon, Daniel awakened the next morning to a warm tongue licking his face. It was Lass! Before he could brace himself, Lad, too, had joined in the fun, burrowing his wet nose in Daniel's shoulder.

"Hey, cut it out!" he whispered, trying not to laugh aloud. "Quiet! You'll wake the others!"

The dogs lay down, content to be petted as Daniel gazed out from under the wagon in which Pauline, Suzannah, and Jamie were still asleep. It was an interesting place in which to wake up.

The sun sent out its pale early rays to rouse the travelers. Soon they began to stir, the men and boys coming out of tents and from under the wagons and making for the creek to dash cold water in their faces.

Meanwhile, the women and older children dressed little ones and began to prepare breakfast.

"Up," Daniel told the dogs. "Time to get up." In the distance, a horse whinnied. It looked like a good day to be heading West, he thought, feeling better about the journey.

In minutes, campfires flared. Mother and Aunt Pearl soon had water from the nearby creek boiling in the big coffeepot. "Give us a few minutes," they said. "We're still trying to get organized."

Suzannah climbed down from the wagon, braiding her hair. Pauline was right behind her, holding onto Jamie, who wiggled and squirmed. "How am I ever going to dress you, pumpkin, if you don't hold still?" she said.

Before long, the smells of coffee and frying bacon filled the crisp morning air. When the men had finished their first mug of coffee, Uncle Karl said, "Let's see to the oxen and the other livestock." Daniel followed the others, glad to see the animals grazing just as they'd left them with Ned Taylor, who had slept in the meadow.

"No sign of Indians," Garth observed.

"Not apt to have trouble with 'em till we cross the Kansas River," Uncle Karl said. "Got to be careful, though."

Daniel helped yoke the oxen and chain them into their teams. "This time," he told his father, "I don't want Marigold in the lead. Tickling under his chin might not work again."

His father chuckled, and Daniel was surprised that he recognized Marigold. "He's this one with more brown spots on his back than the others. Let's put him in the middle."

As they worked, the sun rose fully over the horizon, and the noises of breaking camp grew louder—the shouts of the men digging up tent stakes, the bellow of cattle, the clatter of pots and pans, the barking of dogs, and the jingling of harnesses as oxen were hitched again to the wagons they would pull to the Oregon Territory.

"Morning!" Captain Monroe called as he rode by on his horse. "Appears you folks know what you're doing."

Uncle Karl looked toward Daniel and his father. "Some of us do, 'n' some of us don't."

"We're fast learners," Father assured the captain.

The captain winked at Daniel. "I'd say you are."

When their work was done, they sat down to a breakfast of eggs, bacon, and flapjacks. While they ate, Captain Monroe rode by again. "About a hundred miles from here to the Kansas River ferry, a week's travel." He turned to Uncle Karl, "Once we're underway, I'd like you and a few other Missouri men to act as scouts until we meet up with our guide at the ferry."

Uncle Karl gave a nod of importance. "How about you, Captain? Why ain't you scoutin'?"

"My job's to keep the wagons rolling," he said.

"Fine, then," Uncle Karl replied, taking a last swallow of coffee. "I'll saddle up Gray and come right along."

Garth fetched the saddle from beside their wagon and threw it over the back of his father's gray stallion. "Scout out a good huntin' place for us to camp," he told him.

"Right, boy." Uncle Karl answered and mounted up. As he turned to ride away, he spoke to Daniel and the others. "You take care of them livestock and wagons. Without 'em, we're dead."

"We'll take care of them, don't worry!"

As his uncle rode off, Daniel drew a sigh of relief. At least Uncle Karl would not be breathing down his neck every minute of the day.

When the time to leave neared, the children and dogs raced about, scattering chickens, jumping over butter churns and wagon tongues, and playing hide-and-seek behind the huge wagon wheels. Women called out to each other with excitement as they snuffed out the campfires, while the men checked the harnesses and hitches.

Above the racket, Captain Monroe gave the order at last. "Turn out! Turn out!"

Daniel made sure that Jamie was loosely tied inside the wagon and that Pauline was comfortable. "We're starting out now," he told her as she sketched the scene. "No half-day like yesterday."

"I do hope we'll see Charles soon," she said.

"I hope so for your sake," Daniel agreed. But not for the sake of the wagon train. Charles's gambling had brought nothing but grief everywhere he went. On the other hand, Father always said, "Charles is family, no matter what."

"Your father asked about him at other encampments last night, and a few emigrants said they saw him ride on West with three other men," she said.

"Then he can't be far away."

"No, surely not far." Pauline managed a bright smile for Jamie. "We'll see your father soon," she said, cuddling him close. "And when we get to Oregon, we'll start all over. We'll have a whole new life together."

Her words sounded hopeful, but Daniel thought he had never seen such a sad look on her face.

At the head of the wagon train, Captain Monroe waved his hat in the air. "Wagons, ho-o! Wagons, ho-o!"

A great cheer went up. "Oregon or bust!" called an emigrant.

"Californy, here we come!"

Others fired their rifles in sheer excitement.

The lead wagon began to roll, then one by one, the others followed, their wheels clanking over the dirt path. Suddenly it was time for Garth's wagon, then Father's. A moment later, Daniel snaked his bullwhip in the air, cracking it over the heads of the oxen. "Giddap!" he cried. "Giddap!"

The weight of the oxen's shoulders fell against the yokes once more, and the wagon moved forward. Marigold pulled along with the others, giving no sign of sitting down, at least not yet. Daniel wiped the sweat from his face with a red handkerchief and grinned at Suzannah.

"It's a beautiful day for moving West!" she exclaimed.

"I've never seen a better one!"

A soft rain had fallen during the night, washing the dust from the trees. Now the sun sent down warming rays and dried up the moisture as the wagon train moved across the countryside.

After they had traveled a little way, Suzannah broke the silence. "Wonder if Uncle Karl and Garth will want to go hunting again today."

Daniel shrugged. "Don't know why they would. There's plenty of salt pork and dried beef left."

"Not nearly enough to get to Oregon," she continued. "You may even have to shoot buffalo before we arrive."

He gave her a sidelong glance. Why was she making so much over hunting? Probably she guessed he dreaded the thought of hunting just as much as he hated bullwhacking.

"Boys have all the fun!" she went on crossly. "All I get to do is fetch creek water, collect firewood, and help with the cooking and washing. And I have to wear a blamed sunbonnet while I do it, too!" She untied the strings and retied them loosely, letting her bonnet dangle down her back.

"Your face will turn brown," Daniel warned.

"I don't care one whit!" She stomped her foot and walked on without saying anything more for at least a minute. "How's that Ned Taylor?" she asked.

Daniel gawked at her. "Why do you want to know?"

Suzannah shrugged. "He seems real nice."

"You're not in love with him, are you?" he teased. "Him and his mop of red curls?"

She poked his arm hard. "Are you crazy, Daniel Colton? I'm not in love with anyone. Not likely to be, either!"

He laughed. "I thought maybe that's why you'd tied those ribbons on your braids this morning."

"Hmmmph!" she answered. Then, darting a glance to see if Pauline was listening, she leaned toward Daniel. "I've been wondering why the Taylors would let their son go so far away from home."

"Ned's hired help. The wagon train paid his family for him to come with us."

Suzannah was disgusted. "That's terrible! It's like his family sold him!"

"Seems sad to me, too, but I guess if you're poor and have sixteen children, you need money. Or maybe they just wanted him to have a chance for a better life in Oregon."

"Still seems wrong to me," she said.

All went well during the morning and at their nooning stop. But in the afternoon, several oxen still not broken to the trail lay down in protest, holding up all of the other wagons. Finally, the bullwhackers got them moving again. Daniel was grateful that Marigold behaved herself.

By the time they reached their new campsite in the late afternoon, he was bone-tired. Even the small children didn't play run-sheep-run or romp about the camp as they had yesterday in the meadow.

Uncle Karl rode back to camp and helped unhitch the wagons. "There's wild turkeys all about these parts," he said. "Let's get some for supper. Ned can see to the livestock."

Daniel drew a deep breath. He guessed he couldn't

put it off any longer. It was as good a time as any to try hunting.

When they finished their chores, Daniel got his new rifle from the wagon, then followed the others into the woods. All the way, however, he was thinking about the neighbor boy in Georgetown who had accidentally shot his father while they were hunting.

No sooner had they crossed the creek and stepped from the thicket into the trees, than Uncle Karl put up a hand. "Turkeys! A whole flock of 'em on the ground! Quiet, now. Load your rifles."

Daniel poured the gunpowder down the barrel as he had been taught, dropped in a bullet, then stuffed a wad of packing into the muzzle of his rifle. Next, he jammed the whole thing into place with the ramrod. By the time he finished, he thought, those turkeys would be far away!

Before he could take aim, three shots rang out, and three turkeys settled into the dust. The rest gobbled loudly in distress, and flapped away into the trees.

"Three ain't bad," Uncle Karl said. "We'll have a good supper and plenty left for tomorrow's noonin'." He turned to Daniel. "What happened to you?"

Daniel shrugged uneasily. "By the time I was ready, the other turkeys had flown off."

"They don't fly far," Garth said, starting after them.

"No sense in killing turkeys or other animals we don't need," Father said.

Garth seemed disappointed, but didn't insist.

"Daniel will do more than his part before this journey's over," Father promised. "He always has."

I hope he's right, Daniel thought, wishing his father didn't have to defend him.

When they returned to camp, they found that the women had lit the cookfire and brought a pot of water to boiling. Suzannah sat at the fold-out table cutting up carrots, onions, and potatoes. "Aunt Pearl said it'd probably be a while before you came back, so they've gone off visiting with Jamie."

Uncle Karl scowled, then tossed the dead turkeys by a tree stump. "I'm sure Daniel would be glad to clean and pluck 'em for supper."

"I've never cleaned a turkey—" Daniel began.

Garth snorted. "It figures. Don't know huntin' or trappin'. Don't know how to clean fowl. I'll tell 'im what to do."

While Father and Uncle Karl took the rifles back to their wagons, Garth pointed at the tree stump. "There's a good choppin' block. First, you get the ax and chop off the gobblers' heads. Next, you cut 'em open and pull out the innards. And, last, you dunk 'em in that pot of boilin' water for a minute, then feather 'em."

Daniel's stomach rose up on him, but he swallowed hard and set about the grim task.

"Ain't much of a frontiersman, are you?" Garth said, standing by to see that the job was done right.

"Not yet," Daniel admitted.

It was bad enough to chop off the heads, but then came the scalding stench from dipping the turkeys in boiling water. Daniel gagged and turned his head. Plucking out feathers wasn't much better, so he concentrated on the beautiful colors—green, purple, and bronze. But pulling out the birds' entrails was worst of all. Finally, the grisly job was done, and Daniel darted a glance at his stepcousin.

"Didn't think you could do it," Garth said.

Didn't think I could, either, Daniel thought, his stomach still churning.

Garth's eyes glittered beneath the dark brows. "Can't wait to see you eat them birds."

"Just so I don't have to cook them," Daniel replied

with more bluster than he felt. He grabbed the naked turkeys by their feet and carried them to the fold-out table where Suzannah was cutting up the vegetables.

"Aaugh—" she choked out at the sight of him. "You're all full of blood and feathers."

"Just be glad you didn't have to clean them yourself." He turned on his heel and headed for the stream to wash up. If he never saw another turkey as long as he lived, it would be too soon.

At supper, Daniel filled his tin plate with greens, potatoes, and carrots, but passed up the roasted turkey. Behind him in line, Garth grabbed a drumstick and plopped it on Daniel's plate. "Here," he said with a wicked grin, "to keep up your strength."

"Thank you," Daniel said, trying not to remember where that drumstick had been only a few hours earlier.

At the table, he sat as far as possible from Garth. But he needn't have worried. His stepcousin wasted no time in talk; as usual, he shoveled in the food as fast as he could.

When Lad and Lass settled at Daniel's feet under the table, he quietly slipped the drumstick to them. And when Garth did look up at last, he seemed surprised to find the piece of poultry gone.

Ned Taylor, seated across the table, looked from Daniel's plate to the dogs who were playing with the bone, but wisely said nothing.

The next morning, as soon as it was light enough to see, Daniel pulled out a book. He was lost in the adventures of the Deerslayer when Lad and Lass came to play, and he shushed them, eager to finish a chapter before he was roused for the day's chores.

"Up and at 'em!" Uncle Karl called, much too early to suit Daniel.

Cooking and breaking camp took far less time this morning as the emigrants fell into a routine. Before long, Uncle Karl and the other scouts were riding far ahead.

"We're getting used to wagon life already," Suzannah said, catching up with Daniel.

"Appears like it," he replied as the wagon train rolled through the countryside again. The weather remained fair, and even the most skittish oxen caused no more problems.

At their nooning stop, Mother said, "We'll have turkey stew and cornbread for dinner."

Daniel gulped at the memory of cleaning the turkeys. But he was so hungry by the time it was ready that he ate three bowls of stew and was glad to see Garth looking on.

In the evening, as they settled the wagons and livestock at the new campsite, Uncle Karl rode back from scouting. "Plenty of wild turkeys in the woods here, too. We'd best get us some."

Reluctantly, Daniel got out his rifle and powder horn. *Wonder if I'll ever learn to like hunting,* he thought.

"Get a move on back there, Daniel," Uncle Karl called. "You're holdin' us up."

"Coming," Daniel said, following them across the campground and into the woods.

Since they had gotten a later start this evening, the woods were already dark. The going was rough, too. Brambles pricked at Daniel's pants and shirt, and as he pulled them off he lagged even further behind.

Looking up, he spotted something in a tree. A turkey! It must be a turkey. One thing he knew about turkeys was that they roosted in trees. He also knew that sooner or later he'd have to prove himself as a hunter. Sooner was better, he decided, thinking who would be cleaning the turkeys if he failed again.

He loaded his rifle, sighted down the barrel at the dark mass, then pulled the trigger. But no wild turkey dropped to the ground in front of him. Instead, a cloud of angry hornets burst from their nest.

"Hornets!" he yelled, and took off running.

"Hornets!" he heard Uncle Karl echo. "Run for your lives!"

While Daniel ran off in one direction, they chose another, shrieking like wild men as they thrashed through the underbrush. "Hornets! Run, everyone!"

Daniel raced through the woods, jumped a narrow place in the creek, and headed for the encampment. Now he'd be in real trouble!

Moments later, the others tore out of the woods, a trail of buzzing hornets in pursuit. "Head for the creek!" Uncle Karl shouted. "Stay away from the wagons and livestock!"

The three of them flung their rifles aside, then threw themselves into the creek, ducking their heads under the water. The hornets buzzed just inches above them, then circled the creek twice and a third time for good measure. Finally, they flew back to the woods, and, at long last, Father, Garth, and Uncle Karl climbed out of the creek.

Suzannah did her best to smother her giggles. "They're all drenched to the skin!"

As the three bedraggled hunters approached the wagons, the other emigrants roared with laughter. "Didn't know you fellows could run so fast!" they said. "Best show we seen yet!"

Uncle Karl and Garth glowered, but Father only grinned. "Didn't know I could still run like that myself."

"It was dark and I thought it was a turkey," Daniel explained. "I'm sorry—"

"Not much damage done," Father said. "We didn't

get stung . . . and we all got a much needed bath in the bargain."

"That's the last time I go huntin' with you, Daniel Colton," Uncle Karl announced. "A city feller who don't know a turkey from a hornet's nest ain't got no business carryin' a rifle. From now on, you take care of the livestock while Ned helps with the huntin'." He finally remembered to ask Father. "That agreeable with you, Franklin?"

Father slicked back his wet hair and tried to look serious. "What do you think, son?"

Daniel turned away, feeling disgraced. "Guess I'll take care of the livestock . . . for a few days anyhow," he answered. But there was an ache in his heart and he thought, *Some frontiersman I am!*

CHAPTER
FIVE

The weather had turned stormy by the first of the week when they arrived at the Kansas River. They made camp some distance from the other wagon trains waiting to be ferried across. The falling rain made it more difficult to circle the wagons and hobble the oxen.

Wearing ponchos, Daniel and Suzannah worked steadily to finish up their chores. When they stopped to take a breather, Daniel gazed far beyond the river at the green prairie.

Even with the sun playing hide and seek through the dark clouds, it looked calm and peaceful—a vast, unbroken sea of green grasses. Could dangers really be lurking out there—wild animals, hostile Indians looking for scalps, starvation, even death? It didn't seem likely.

"What do you see?" Suzannah asked.

Daniel shook his head. "Nothing much. Looks about the same on the other side of the river, but after a ways, there are no trees. Not a one. Guess that's why it's called prairie."

Garth came up behind them. "That's Indian Territory."

Daniel felt a sudden chill as he recalled something else Garth had said: *I'm goin' to get me an Indian.*

"Don't see any sign of 'em now," Garth continued. "Except them poor excuses runnin' the ferry. Can hardly call 'em Indians, though."

Daniel felt a little disappointed himself. "They don't look like mighty warriors, if that's what you mean." He knew these were Shawnee and Delaware Indians. They were dressed in tattered calico shirts, buckskin trousers, and moccasins.

No sooner had they settled in the wagon circle than they were greeted by a strange creature riding a brown-spotted Indian pony. A wispy white beard hung halfway to the man's belt, and long white hair streamed from beneath a broad-brimmed hat squashed flat on his head. He was wearing old buckskins that looked as if he had lived in them forever.

"Name's Mordechai!" he called as he waved them together. "Don't ask fer a last name, 'cause I don't own one. And don't ask my horse's name, cause he don't own one, neither. You can call him No-Name if you want."

Mordechai eyed the emigrants' soggy camp. "At least you brought oxen fer pullin' the wagons. Injuns ain't got much use fer 'em. And oxen make out on prairie grass when horses and mules can't."

Captain Monroe hurried forward to greet the guide. "Let me introduce you—"

"Plenty of time fer that later," Mordechai said, still astride his pony. "What's important is you get these wagons fixed proper. Ain't no promise at all that them Injuns won't cross the river tonight and attack."

One of the emigrants said, "But we're not in Indian Territory yet."

Mordechai shook his head. "Greenhorns all think the same—that over here is yer land and 'crost the Kansas is Injun Country. But them Injuns figger it's *all* theirs."

"But the treaty—" someone said.

"They don't cotton much to treaties," Mordechai interrupted. "And they ain't dumb, neither. They can see we're a'comin', cain't they? I got us a half-Injun guide, White Feather, to help us on t'other side. Now let's git these wagons set up right now in a proper circle."

He put them all to work. Every wagon tongue had to overlap the next wagon. And the rear wheel hub of each wagon must be chained to the front wheel hub of the wagon behind it. When they had finished the chore to Mordechai's satisfaction, the men found they had formed a tight corral. Daniel helped picket the horses to stakes to prevent stealing.

"Now," Mordechai said, "we need four men to keep watch in four-hour shifts. I got a lot to teach you greenhorns, and I aim to start now."

"Whew!" Suzannah sighed. "He sounds like a slave-driver."

"But he sounds like a guide we can trust," Daniel said. "We'll be a lot safer if we do what he says. Captain Monroe told us that Mordechai was once a mountain man and lived with the Indians, so he knows what it takes to make it all the way to Oregon."

"Looks to me like he's got himself crazy, livin' with them Indians," Garth muttered.

"I agree with Daniel. We'll be safer now," said Ned, who had heard everything.

"What do *you* know?" Garth asked Ned. "You're only hired help."

"I've lived in Missouri all my life," Ned replied, "if that counts for anythin'."

Garth didn't reply, since he was a Missourian himself.

Nearby, Mordechai and the captain were talking. "Got any troublemakers amongst you?" the old man asked.

Daniel couldn't make out all of Captain Monroe's answer, only that they had agreed to no drinking, no gambling, and no traveling on the Sabbath.

To Daniel's amazement, Mordechai agreed. "Good idees," the old trapper said, "as long as we get over them mountains afore the snow hits."

When Daniel opened his eyes the next morning, he found that most of the family was up ahead of him. Mother, Father, and Suzannah were standing around his bunk under the wagon, waiting to wish him a happy birthday.

"Birthday?" He slipped out of his bedroll, suddenly wide awake. *Thirteen!* Today he was thirteen years old—no longer a boy, but beginning on manhood.

"I brought some fruitcake from home for your birthday," Mother said. "And I made a new shirt for you—a yellow one. Thought you'd be growing a lot on this trip."

In the early morning light, his mother's hair gleamed like gold and her round face was so full of love that he couldn't help hugging her, no matter how old he was.

Looking on, Father cleared his throat and put out his hand. "A milestone, son," he said, his eyes suspiciously moist. But when Daniel took his hand, instead of shaking it, his father pulled him into his strong arms. "Hope you're not too old for a man-sized hug. I'm proud to have you for my son."

Suzannah rolled her eyes and made a face. "And I'm glad to have you for a cousin . . . usually. I got you some new fishhooks, and Pauline has something for you, too."

Pauline poked her head out the wagon flap and handed out a delicate watercolor. "I thought you'd like this to remember our stay in Independence."

"Why, you painted me climbing out of the wagon at Aunt Pearl's house," Daniel said. "And you've made me look good, too. Thanks, Pauline. Thank you, everyone."

At that moment, Mordechai limped into the wagon circle. "Sun's up! Let's hit the trail!"

As the other emigrants emerged from their wagons and bedrolls, Mordechai added, "Ain't time fer breakfast. Hustle, or we'll miss our place in line fer the ferry."

In moments, everyone was on the move. Under Mordechai's direction, the oxen were yoked and hitched to the wagons in record time. Before long the wagons were lined up facing the Kansas River, one behind the other, waiting their turn to cross.

"I don't like the looks of that broken-down rope ferry," Daniel told Suzannah. "And I don't like having to swim the livestock across. What if they don't make it?"

Suzannah shrugged. "We don't have much choice, I guess."

Mordechai rode up alongside. "You there," he said, squinting at Daniel, "you a good horseman?"

"I haven't ridden much," Daniel admitted.

"You stay with the wagon and the women then," he was told. "And make sure the shims are under the wagon wheels good."

"But—" Daniel began to protest, but it was too late. The guide was already riding on, assigning tasks to the others. Ned, Garth, Father, and Uncle Karl would help swim the cattle, while he, Daniel Meriwether Colton, who was now thirteen years old, had to stay with the women and children! His mother would be in charge of their lead wagon, Suzannah of the second, and he of the third wagon. It's a wonder Mordechai didn't ask Pauline or Jamie to take charge of theirs, he fumed.

His mother must have noticed his agggravation, for she came by with a big piece of fruitcake. "It may be the only time you'll ever have birthday cake for breakfast," she said, "but I won't let you start out your birthday on an empty stomach."

As if things weren't bad enough, Daniel felt his eyes cloud up, and his voice cracked as he thanked her.

His mother patted his shoulder, then moved on to find Pauline and Jamie. "I'll give some to the others, too. Just remember, your day as a grown-up will come all too soon."

Daniel nodded miserably. He sure wasn't a grown-up today. He gazed at the river as he ate the fruitcake. At least the cake was his favorite—moist and full of nuts, honey, and raisins.

"Look at that!" Suzannah cried.

The wagon train ahead of them was now crossing the river on a raftlike ferry made of logs tied together. Ropes of buffalo hide were used to pull the contraption from one side to the other. Downstream, oxen and cattle bawled in the muddy water as they struggled against the fierce current, the men on horseback doing their best to keep the herd together. Daniel could see that a few of the oxen, swept downriver, were being lassoed and pulled ashore.

His mother passed him as she returned to the front wagon. "Mordechai says it must have rained hard up north, the way the river is rushing," she said. "Look, it's all they can do to move the livestock across."

When the first wagon train had regrouped across the river, the log ferry returned to their side.

"Move them wagons and be quick about it!" Mordechai bellowed.

At the head of the line, the Murphys had already unhitched the oxen from their three wagons. The men pushed the first two onto the dilapidated ferry, and Daniel watched the Indians shim the wagon wheels against the logs. They were doing a good job of it. Old Mordechai had just told him to check so he'd feel useful, he thought.

Once the Murphys' first two wagons were firmly positioned aboard the ferry, the Indians shouted to the ferrymen to start pulling the rope to the far riverbank.

"Get that livestock into the water! Move 'em fast afore they get skeered by the current!" Mordechai yelled.

Mr. Murphy and his older sons drove the oxen into the river. "Swim boys!" they shouted. "Swim fer shore!"

There was an anxious moment when Zeke Murphy had to lasso a floundering ox and pull him ashore, but the Murphys' first two wagons, quickly followed by the third, crossed the Kansas River into Indian Territory more smoothly than Daniel thought possible.

One by one, the wagons in front of Daniel's were loaded and ferried across the rushing water. And almost before he knew it, Father and the other menfolk had unhitched the oxen and helped the Indians roll Mother's and Aunt Pearl's wagons onto the ferry.

Daniel was still unhitching his own oxen when Garth and Uncle Karl came to swim them across. Daniel found himself standing at the front of the line. Before him, the empty log ferry bobbed back across the churning water. His throat was suddenly dry. What if he couldn't do it?

"Next wagon!" shouted Mordechai.

Daniel jumped onto the raft with the Indians and felt it tilt beneath his feet. As he regained his balance, he saw that the Indians had sprung forward to ease the wagon onto the logs, and he grabbed the wagon tongue to help. Quickly they shimmed the wheels—wedging blocks of wood underneath to keep them from rolling into the water.

He straightened and turned, almost slipping on a log and falling overboard. He backed up, his stomach lurching, embarrassed to see that the Indians had noticed.

While he waited, Daniel checked the shims under all four of his wagon wheels. Despite the log flooring, they were as tight as could be.

Suddenly one of the Indians gave a shout, and the ferry began the crossing. The raft, loaded with the two heavy wagons, rode low in the water. Daniel grabbed a wagon wheel and held on, turning to watch the men on horseback battling the river.

Father, Uncle Karl, and Garth had their hands full with the livestock. Mid-river, the current grew stronger. As one of the oxen drifted away from the herd, Uncle Karl swung his lasso expertly and snagged the animal around the neck, pulling him toward the far riverbank.

Then it was Marigold, thrashing in the swift current and bawling in terror. While Uncle Karl tugged the first ox to safety, Father pulled out his lariat and swung it wide, missing Marigold on the first try. Again he swung and missed. By this time, Marigold was well downstream.

But Father urged his horse forward, swinging the thin rope over his head once more. This time, the noose settled snugly over Marigold's horns, and Father pulled him to shore.

Swimming his horse across the river behind them, Garth shouted and struck the rest of the oxen with his bullwhip, while Ned brought up the rear with Elsa, the milk cow, who had balked at the raging torrent. It had taken Ned all this time just to get her into the water. Now she drifted away just out of his reach.

Elsa's soft brown eyes were wide with terror as the current caught her, and Ned swung his lariat. It whizzed past the cow, just missing her head.

Seeing Ned's predicament, Garth swung his horse around and swam back to help. Just as he reached Elsa, his horse collided with Ned's in the water. Whinnying wildly, Ned's horse tossed him into the mud-churned river.

"Help!" yelled Ned just before he went under.

Daniel watched in horror from the ferry. Ned fought the current, floundering in the water as he was carried downstream. Father and Uncle Karl were still struggling to bring the oxen to shore, and Garth was doing his best to bring in the two horses. Busy with their own emergencies, they didn't see Ned's predicament.

There's no one else to help Ned, came a small voice. *It's up to you, Daniel.* Never had he felt such a powerful urge.

Daniel pulled off his soggy shoes and dove into the cold water, swimming as fast as he could. The current was stronger than any he had ever experienced in the Potomac River back home. But there was no turning back now.

Swimming with all of his might, he looked around and finally saw Ned when he surfaced a good distance away. Ned saw him coming, his eyes wild with fear.

"Here, Ned . . . grab on!" Daniel yelled. "Grab my arm!"

But Ned grabbed his neck, pulling both of them under the muddy water. As they came up, Daniel choked and tried to shake Ned off. He'd heard about drowning people who, in their desperation, took their rescuers down with them. He knew what he had to do.

Pulling one arm free, Daniel slugged Ned on the chin. Ned blinked once, sagged, and fell backwards into the water. Instantly, Daniel grabbed him by his red hair and swam for shore. *Lord, help me,* he prayed over and over. *Lord, help me—*

By the time they reached the riverbank, Daniel was so exhausted he could barely stand.

"Hold on!" his father yelled, splashing over to help.

"I . . . I had to hit him—" Daniel gasped.

"Don't talk now, son. Catch your breath first." His father and Uncle Karl lifted Ned and carried him to the riverbank.

Dazed, Ned shook his head, coughing and choking on river water. Finally he came around.

"You all right, Ned?" Father asked.

Ned coughed again. "I am . . . now."

"Well, Daniel," his father said when he and Ned were wrapped in blankets from one of the wagons. "Guess you'll never forget your thirteenth birthday."

Lightheaded himself, Daniel could scarcely take it all in. "What about . . . Marigold and . . . Elsa?"

Father leaned back his head and laughed. "The ox and the milk cow? Why, they're both in a lot better shape than you and Ned are!"

Ned ran a hand through his damp curls. "I reckon I owe you my life," he said to Daniel.

"You don't owe me anything . . . except maybe a punch on my chin. I expect yours might swell up some."

Just then Mordechai rode up on No-Name and dismounted. "I heerd 'ain't no greater love than thet a man lay down his life fer another.'" He squinted at Daniel. "But I ain't never knowed a flesh-and-blood man who done it."

Curious, Father asked, "Where did you hear that . . . about a man laying down his life?"

"Used to be a mountain man, a trapper jest like me, named Jedediah Smith," the old man replied. "He blazed the trail 'crost the Rockies in '26, when no one thought the mountains could be crossed from the East."

Mordechai scratched his chin. "The trappers called him 'Bible-totin' Jed.' Didn't smoke, chew 'backy, swear, or drink spirits, but many's the time he read to us from the Good Book. I didn't think much on it then, but I do now." He turned to Daniel. "This young feller puts me in mind of Jedediah . . . and what Christ said about layin' down yer life fer another like He done fer us."

"I prayed," Daniel said. "I prayed for help."

"I prayed for you myself," Father said.

A stillness fell on them, and Daniel remembered the voice that had urged him to save Ned from drowning. In the silence, even the prairie birds stopped twittering. It seemed as if God spoke in the quiet. And Daniel knew now that whatever dangers he must face in this Indian Territory, God was traveling right along with them.

He had been plenty scared, all right. But maybe being a real man didn't mean not being afraid. Maybe being a real man meant doing the right thing—even when you were scared!

CHAPTER
SIX

The crowd of emigrants who had gathered some distance down the trail cheered when they saw Daniel and Ned Taylor riding double behind Father and Mordechai.

"The young feller's purely a hero!" one man called.

"You saved that boy's life!" a woman declared. "I saw the whole thing as we crossed over on the ferry!"

Daniel glowed under their praise. Being known as someone who'd saved a life sure beat being known as the boy who tickled oxen under the chin and shot at hornets' nests. He tried to smile modestly as he dismounted from behind his father, but his legs were so wobbly that he stumbled and nearly fell.

His mother came running from their wagon. "Oh, Daniel, we never prayed so hard!"

He nodded, glad when the attention turned to Ned, who was still white-faced from his ordeal.

"Ned Taylor needs to ride in a wagon this mornin'," Mordechai said. "Daniel, too."

"Daniel can take my place," his mother said. "I'd much rather walk than be jounced about anyhow."

"We'll take Ned," Aunt Pearl said, ignoring her new husband's frown.

Suzannah offered to drive Daniel's wagon. "Just till he rests up a little."

Mordechai agreed. "We done better'n most so far. Only lost one cow to the river. I seen more'n a dozen cattle go down at one crossin' . . . and plenty of greenhorns drowned, too." He looked at the river with respect as the last of their wagons were ferried across. "Let's get this here wagon train movin'!" he hollered.

"We ain't had time for breakfast," someone complained.

"Eat yer dry biscuits!" he retorted. "We got to be through them mountains afore snow sets in, or you'll *really* know what it is to be hungry!"

Everyone ran for their wagons, eager now to start the trek through the prairie, even if they had to eat stale soda biscuits for breakfast. Fortunately, most of the oxen were already yoked and hitched up.

Daniel's mother slipped him another piece of fruitcake. "You've already had a birthday to remember. But here's something to hold you until our nooning."

He took the cake gratefully and climbed into the wagon, while Mother poked her head inside to be sure he was comfortable among the barrels, crates, and dangling skillets. "We're thanking the Lord that He saw fit to save two lives today," she said.

Daniel wanted to tell her about that moment when he knew he was to jump into the river to save Ned . . . and the moment afterwards on the riverbank when he'd felt God's nearness. But he didn't know where to begin. Instead, he smiled and settled back against the quilts.

Outside, Captain Monroe shouted, "Wagons, ho!"

"Sleep well," his mother said, and climbed down.

As the wagons rolled on beyond the Kansas River, Daniel glanced out the back hole in the canvas. Nearby were a few great oak trees and under them, wooden grave markers. He read: "Andrew Timmons, January 5, 1798— May 4, 1845. Dead in Christ on the way to Oregon." A fresh grave was marked, "Lucy Mitchell, June 30, 1820— May 9, 1848. At home with the Lord."

Not everyone made it across the Kansas River. In fact, from what he'd heard, quite a few people died on every wagon train crossing the wilderness. Closing his eyes, he prayed, *I thank Thee, Lord, that Ned Taylor wasn't one of them.*

When the wagon train halted for their nooning, Daniel climbed out groggily.

"You don't look like a hero—not with your hair standing up like a wild man," Suzannah teased.

Daniel combed it back with his fingers, giving his cowlick an extra pat for good measure. "How's Ned?"

Suzannah jerked a thumb toward Aunt Pearl's wagon. "He looks about as sleepy as you do."

Ned was climbing down from the wagon, rubbing his eyes. When he saw Daniel, he headed over. "I was thinkin' when I woke up . . . no matter what you say, I owe you my life."

Daniel shook his head. "You owe your life to God— not to me or anyone else."

"Is that why you done it . . . why you saved me from drowning?"

Daniel remembered the small voice from within that had so clearly directed him. "Yes. I—"

But Garth, coming up behind them, interrupted. "Well, if it ain't the hero! Don't you think you're somethin'?"

"Why should I?" Daniel asked, but Garth only shot him a hateful look and hurried past.

"I think you surprised him," Suzannah said. "Garth probably thought you'd be stuck up by now about it."

Daniel watched her as she left to fetch firewood, thinking about what she'd said. Then he turned to Ned. "Guess we'd better see how the livestock are doing."

When they unhitched the oxen and led them to the side of the trail to graze, Daniel realized how much the terrain had changed while he'd slept. Instead of woodlands or even occasional trees, there was only tall green grass and a great blue dome of sky overhead.

"The prairie looks different, not like I expected," he said. "I've never seen such flat country."

Ned looked out over the landscape that stretched on as far as the eye could see. "Indian country."

"I know. And Garth plans to kill himself one."

Ned's eyes widened. "He'll bring trouble on all of us. Then again, maybe he's just talkin'."

"Maybe . . . but I think he means it."

The two boys worked on in silence, thinking about the unknown dangers not only ahead of them, but right in their own camp.

For their nooning, there were wild greens, applesauce, roasted prairie chickens, and hot buttered cornbread.

Daniel was starved and ate heartily. As he finished his third helping of cornbread, a horse and rider galloped in from the west. Even from a distance, he recognized the man at once.

"It's Charles!" Pauline cried out. She ran through the tall prairie grasses to meet him.

But Suzannah only rolled her eyes, and Daniel knew she was thinking of all the trouble her sister's no-good husband had given them on the stagecoach trip to Independence.

When Charles slid off Lucky, they could see that the stallion's chestnut coat was covered with foamy lather and that Charles himself was gasping for breath. "Indians . . . they got the others! I was the only one who escaped!"

Mordechai shook his head. "Don't pay fer greenhorns to go ridin' out a few at a time like thet. Indians prize good hosses, and they know how to get 'em." The old man frowned. "Let this be a lesson to the rest of you not to stray off. Even if you ain't got a good hoss, they're apt to hold you fer ransom."

"Ransom?" Daniel echoed. "You mean they'd make someone buy us back?"

"'Zackly," Mordechai said. "And they'd want a right smart amount of gold fer a sturdy young feller like yerself—'specially one who's passed a test fer bravery."

Daniel drew a deep breath. He hadn't felt brave at all back at the river. And now he seemed to be struggling once again with his old enemy, fear. If he were ever captured, he thought, paying a ransom would be a bitter hardship for his family, but it would be a sight better than becoming a slave to the Indians.

Father stepped up. "Charles, I'll take care of Lucky for you. What you need right now is food and rest."

Charles nodded, still panting for breath. "I've been

lost for days. Then when I saw the smoke from your cookfires, I thought—"

Pauline's blue eyes brimmed with concern. "Let me help you into the wagon, dear, then I'll get you something to eat and drink."

Surprisingly, Charles allowed her to help him without a word of protest. And as the wagon train moved on, he slept all afternoon and straight through the night.

Daniel couldn't help wondering if Charles would take his rightful place as bullwhacker for his family's wagon after he'd rested up. But the next day, Mordechai appointed him to be a flanking rider alongside the wagon train, and Daniel had his old job back.

"About two hundred miles to the Platte River," Mordechai announced. "Nigh onto two weeks' travel, if we're lucky."

They were joined by their half-Indian scout who spoke to Mordechai, then rode off without a word to anyone else. "White Feather'll be scoutin' out ahead fer good water and grass . . . and fer bad Injuns," the old guide explained.

Despite the constant threat of trouble, each day seemed to blend into the next. The trail began to shift toward the northwest, and the prairie seemed less flat than before. As they rolled along, the land rose and fell in gentle swells, much like a vast green ocean. Riding the crest of these "waves" were the white-topped wagons. With their slow swaying and billowing canvas "sails," Daniel understood why the covered wagons were called prairie schooners.

Here, too, were acres and acres of wildflowers. Suzannah spent hours plaiting them into colorful necklaces. After she had covered herself and Jamie with them, she twined them about the oxen's horns, much to Daniel's dismay.

Once, they spotted great fields of clover, alive with hummingbirds hovering above the pink and white blossoms. All of nature appeared to be putting on its most spectacular show for the travelers. And since the river crossing, even the rains waited until nighttime to fall, when Daniel slept with Lad and Lass in a black India-rubber tent under the wagon.

But in spite of the beauty surrounding them each day, the threat they were facing was never far from their minds. In the evenings, Mordechai insisted on tighter corrals. "Can't be too keerful in Injun Territory," he warned.

The first glimpse of their dreaded enemies came one morning before the first rays of sunlight had pierced the eastern sky. "Indians!" someone shouted. "Indians!"

Daniel peered out from under the wagon. In the gray dawn, a hundred or more braves had gathered not far from the wagon train. Bearing lances, shields, and bows, they were mounted on sturdy ponies. Red paint streaked their faces, and their dark hair bristled with feathers.

Daniel rolled out of his bedroll fast—toward the inner circle of the wagons. Around him, women clutched their babies, and the small children cried and hid under quilts in the wagons.

"Load your rifles, men! Now!" ordered Captain Monroe.

Shaken, Daniel grabbed his flintlock and followed his father.

"We'll be praying!" Daniel's mother told them as they passed her on the way to join the other men.

"No shootin'!" Mordechai said. "These here is Osage and Kansas. Let me handle 'em. Men, stand back with yer rifles. And don't get trigger happy, or I'll blow you to kingdom come myself!"

Swallowing his fear, Daniel stepped over a wagon

tongue behind Mordechai, who was shouting something to the band of Indians in their native language.

Please, Lord, prayed Daniel, *don't let there be a fight. I don't want to kill anyone.*

Hardly daring to breathe, he watched as the chief advanced on foot with a white flag. The Indian, wrapped in a colorful blanket and wearing a huge headdress of feathers, was tall and walked proudly. As the sun's first rays brightened the prairie behind him, he appeared even more fearsome to Daniel.

"Stay back, men, and no shootin'," Mordechai reminded them, then limped forward to meet the chief, his wispy white hair and beard blowing in the early morning breeze. They met halfway between the gathering of Indians and the wagon train. Shortly, the chief called out six Indian men and squaws.

"They want to trade buffalo skins and moccasins fer beads 'n such," Mordechai announced. "Tell the women to break out their goods. Men, put down yer rifles."

Garth, standing beside Daniel, hesitated for a long time before lowering his rifle. Nearby, Ned Taylor looked as relieved as Daniel felt. They wouldn't have to shoot, at least not yet.

Before long, the women brought out the goods they had been told to bring for trading—beads, mirrors, scissors, ribbons, jackknives, and colorful calico shirts. Daniel noticed that Suzannah and his mother and aunt were among them. Mordechai waved them forward and stayed to oversee the trading.

After a while, Suzannah returned, waving a pair of moccasins. "It's too hot to wear these infernal high-topped shoes!"

"You'll look like a squaw!" Daniel teased.

"I don't care," she retorted. "I'd rather look like a

squaw than for my feet to hurt for two thousand miles! You and Garth ought to try these yourselves."

"Not me!" Garth said. "I wouldn't wear their filth."

Daniel wondered what Garth might say when both Aunt Pearl and Mother brought back buffalo blankets. It didn't take long for his stepcousin to notice. "You couldn't get me to sleep under one of them things. Probably crawlin' with lice."

"You'll be glad for the warmth if we have to cross the high mountains in the snow," Aunt Pearl said quietly.

Garth scowled. "Then I'd sooner freeze!"

Aunt Pearl shook her head sadly, but said no more.

When the trading ended, the Indians were escorted back to their party. Soon they were riding off behind the high prairie grasses in the distance.

"Strange how they just seem to appear and disappear," Daniel observed.

Mordechai overheard his remark. "No doubt we seem jest as strange to them, ridin' outta nowhere in our white wagons, trespassin' on their land."

As the wagon train got underway once more, Daniel said to Suzannah, "It's hard for me to remember we're in Indian Territory."

"At least you *try to* remember," Suzannah replied. "There are others around here who don't."

"Like Garth," he said.

She nodded. "When we came back from trading, he was glaring at the Indians so fiercely, it scared me."

Two wagons ahead, Garth was cracking his whip even more savagely than usual. What made his stepcousin so angry? What had the Indians ever done to him?

Just then Charles rode by, without so much as a glance in their direction. He'd made an amazing recovery after his escape from the Indians. But, instead of being grateful that his life had been spared, as Daniel had hoped,

Charles was again filled with self-importance. The man who had gambled away Suzannah's and Pauline's home and belongings hadn't changed a bit.

"I wonder why Pauline married him," he asked.

Suzannah shrugged. "Probably because he was the handsomest man she'd ever seen. Besides, he was really nice to her . . . at least, while they were courting. Then, when our parents died, I think she needed someone to take care of her—of *us*. Of course, she didn't know about his gambling then."

As they walked beside the oxen, Daniel recalled something his father had often said. He said, "It's letting a little sin—like gambling—take root, then grow and grow until it takes over completely that can ruin a man like Charles. That's why we pray 'deliver us from temptation and keep us from evil.' "

Suzannah gave him a curious look. "Why, Daniel Meriwether Colton, you sound just like a preacher!"

He grinned. "Maybe I do. It's just that I'm beginning to understand Charles. You know, I even feel a little sorry for him. It's like some evil has taken over his life, and he doesn't know what to do about it. But I still don't know why *Garth* is so bitter."

Suzannah pondered his words for a long time before she replied. "Well, there is one thing sure. There's plenty of danger ahead without the two of them causing more trouble. We could all get scalped . . . or the wagons could overturn, or even roll down a mountain—"

"There's danger ahead all right," he agreed, looking out over the endless green prairie. "Anything could happen before we reach the Oregon Territory. Anything."

CHAPTER
SEVEN

As the wagon train moved on day after day, only small groups of Indians came to trade buffalo robes and moccasins. When Daniel saw them up close, he was surprised to find that most of the men's heads were shaved except for greased scalp locks. But there were no more large war parties waving spears and lances.

One morning five Indians approached the wagons to trade, spreading out their moccasins and deerskin shirts on a buffalo robe. When they spoke, Mordechai translated. "They want beads and calico shirts in exchange."

All of a sudden, Garth raised his rifle and took aim at one of the Indians. They all froze, not moving a muscle.

"Garth—" Father warned.

The boy paid him no attention, but kept the barrel of his gun trained on the brave's shaved head.

"God tells us not to kill," Father continued quietly, "no matter what reasons we think we might have for it."

"Then why doesn't your God tell *them* that?" Garth spat out the words.

"We don't know all the answers, but I do know that some of His rules are very clear."

Garth glanced at Father for an instant. "Like what?"

"'Thou shalt not kill,'" Father quoted. "It's one of His Ten Commandments. Now put down your rifle, son."

Garth thought on it, then slowly lowered the rifle. "I'll do it. But only because my ma used to say so, too."

Everyone breathed more easily, and the Indians backed away, then leaped on their horses and disappeared over the horizon.

When they stopped for the day, Daniel asked his mother, "Why does Garth hate Indians so much?"

Mother sighed. "Because a drunken Indian killed his mother on their farm in Missouri."

"Killed his mother?"

She nodded. "While she was hanging the wash out on the clothesline." Her blue eyes filled with pain. "It'd be a hard thing to live with, wouldn't it?"

Daniel felt a little dizzy, thinking how he'd feel if an Indian killed Mother or Father, or one of the others. Something like that wouldn't be easy to forgive.

At supper, Mordechai asked Father and Charles to lend a hand with the scouting, which left Mother to drive the oxen. "The poor old things are used to the prairie by now. They won't be any trouble," she said.

"If the oxen lay down," Garth put in, "you can always get Daniel to tickle them under the chin."

Mother smiled, and Daniel laughed, even though he knew Garth meant to anger him. Better to be taunted than to be puffed up with pride for being a hero, he thought. Besides, now he understood his stepcousin's bitterness.

As they rode on, no one was as worried about Indians as they were about what Garth might do when he saw them. Besides, there were stream crossings to be concerned about. The heavy spring rains had made the waters treacherous.

When they passed one wagon train, though, the captain called out, "We hear there's raiding Pawnees in these parts."

Mordechai waved it aside. "Jest talk. Them Pawnees ain't got their strength back from the smallpox some years back. Besides, we got more scouts to watch fer 'em now."

Next came the "turn-backs." In a single day, three families who had dropped out of wagon trains ahead, passed by. *We've turned back,* said the grim looks on their faces. *We're going back home, and we don't want to talk about it.*

"What happened?" Daniel asked. "Why'd they turn back?"

"Some lose their stock to poisoned water," Mordechai explained. "Some lose their beef cattle and saddle horses to Indians. That's the lucky ones. The unlucky ones lose some in their fam'lies to the fever 'n accidents, or lose mothers and young'uns when they're a'bornin'." He waited for his words to sink in. "This ain't no Sunday outin'."

"Couldn't we spare them a few provisions?" Mother suggested.

"We'll need every bit of our food afore we're done," Mordechai objected. "They can make it back by huntin'. They's plenty of rabbits and prairie chickens hereabouts."

Late one afternoon they came upon an abandoned wagon that loomed like a ghost on the grassy prairie. Daniel eyed the circling vultures.

"What do you suppose happened?" Suzannah asked.

"Sickness," Daniel guessed. "Maybe they died of

ague and fever, and then the Indians came later for the horses and cattle."

Skirting the wagon, they saw newly dug graves, a silent reminder that death also stalked the trail. "Then who dug the graves?" Suzannah asked fearfully.

"Probably another wagon train came along and buried them."

At that moment Mordechai broke into their thoughts. "What you lollygaggin' fer? There's miles to go afore we kin rest!"

A good thing they weren't camping nearby, Daniel decided. Not after seeing the "turn-backs" and the abandoned wagons and graves. "Mordechai's wise to move us on, even if it's our stopping time for the evening," he told Suzannah. "It's not smart to make camp next to an abandoned wagon and fresh graves."

They moved uneasily into a bold orange sunset.

The next day brought no surprises, and they were able to make good time before they stopped for the day. While Suzannah and the other young women and children gathered brush for cookfires, Daniel and the bullwhackers looked after their oxen, cleaning out sore hooves and leading them to a nearby creek for water. Then there were the wagon repairs, and greasing axles and wheel spindles. Since Garth rode out with the hunting parties, Daniel had to keep up all three family wagons, and the work seemed endless. Not that Garth was a slacker, for he often rode back with rabbits and antelopes tied to the flanks of his horse.

When Ned finished his own chores, he came to help. "Garth's about the best shot of all the hunters," he remarked.

Daniel nodded. "He should be. He practices a lot."

"It worries me some, though," Ned said.

"Me, too. I think he likes shooting too much. Or maybe it's just because I don't care for it at all."

By noon the next day the wagons reached Platte River country, a great treeless land except by the river, where cottonwoods and willow trees grew. Wagon wheels screeched over the dry stretches of land, sending up a thick cloud of dust. For days they traveled along the sprawling river.

At their wagon train meeting one night, Daniel learned an interesting fact. "In German, the word *platte* means 'flat,'" said Mr. Amptmann.

"And flatlands they are!" everyone agreed.

"It's getting just plain dreary, if you ask me!" Suzannah complained.

Mr. Murphy, who had a talent for making up jolly songs, took out his fiddle and played while he sang:

> *There's not a log to make a seat*
> *Along the River Platte,*
> *So when you eat you've got to stand*
> *Or sit down square and flat.*

Everyone laughed, and Daniel asked Captain Monroe, "When will we be crossing the Platte?"

"Not till we come to a shallow place," replied the captain. "Don't worry, though. Mordechai and our Indian scout have crossed this river more than once."

"I wasn't worried for myself," Daniel assured him. "Ned?"

Daniel nodded. "After almost drowning once already, the Platte can't look very good to him."

Captain Monroe patted his shoulder. "You're what a man calls a real friend."

It was a fine thing to hear, Daniel mused, but it didn't change matters. With Father, Charles, and Uncle Karl scouting ahead and Garth out hunting, Daniel was the only man in their family most days . . . except for Jamie, who didn't help a bit.

As they moved on, there were fewer and fewer trees, not even willows or cottonwoods for their cookfires. Some of the emigrants found dried buffalo droppings to burn, but Mother and Aunt Pearl refused to cook over them.

Suzannah stuck her nose in the air, too. "You won't see *me* picking up 'buffalo chips'!"

"You'll change yer mind if you git hungry enough!" Mordechai said when he heard their complaints.

When they began to see slick mud sloughs where the huge buffalo rolled to cool themselves, Mordechai said, "Afore long, we'll be seein' the big fellers themselves."

The very next evening, the hunting party shot three buffalo, and the entire camp ate steak, a welcome change from beans and cornbread. After supper, Mordechai showed them how to smoke the leftover meat over the cookfires. "It'll be tough, like all jerked meat, but you'll be glad to have it afore long," he promised.

Most nights, everyone was too tired for music, and Daniel often lay awake long after the others were sleeping and listened to the wolves howl. Now the best part of the journey was Sundays, when they had a morning worship service and a whole afternoon to rest.

Continuing along the Platte River for many days, it still came as a surprise the morning Mordechai said, "We'll be fordin' the river right here."

"Here?" Daniel asked, eyeing the South Fork of the Platte. "Now, while my wagon's first in line?"

Pauline sounded equally uncertain. "Isn't there a ferry to take the wagons across?"

"Won't find no more ferries," Mordechai replied.

"It's the widest place we've seen yet. At least a mile to the other side," called one man. "Can't we find a narrower place?"

"The wider, the better. Usually means shallow water," Mordechai explained. "I'll ride over 'n back jest to prove it. While I'm at it, water the livestock aplenty so's they don't stop to drink while they're crossin'."

"What about quicksand?" someone yelled.

"That's why you want to water the livestock first and keep 'em movin'." Mordechai started No-Name into the water. "If they stop to drink mid-river, they'll mire down."

Daniel drew a deep breath and tugged his oxen toward the water. They could sink. They could sink and be gone.

While the emigrants watered the livestock, they watched Mordechai ride his Indian pony slowly across the mile-long stretch of river. The water reached no higher than No-Name's saddle, a reassuring sight.

When Mordechai rode back, he wasted no time. "Daniel, climb up in that driver's seat and git them oxen across. When you git on the other side, move your team and wagon away so's the others kin come on out. Then head 'em up behind you in a line."

Daniel hesitated, and Mordechai called, *"Now!"*

He clambered up to the driver's seat, breathed a quick prayer, then cracked the bullwhip above the heads of the team. "Giddup, boys! Giddup! Gee!"

Astride No-Name, Mordechai helped lead Daniel's reluctant oxen to the river's edge and into the water. "Jest remember the old sayin', 'The Platte's too thick to drink and too thin to plow.'"

The idea only reminded Daniel of quicksand. He

clung to the driver's seat, with Pauline and Jamie riding behind him in the wagon.

"Giddup, boys! Giddup!" He snapped the whip again as the oxen lumbered into the water. Ripples flowed out from around them as they moved along, the water rising higher and higher. After a while, when the river reached the hubs of the wagon wheels, it seemed as if they were floating in the midst of a great sea.

"I can't swim, either," Pauline said, tears in her eyes. "If . . . if there's trouble, promise you'll save Jamie."

"No one's going to have to swim this time," Daniel replied, sounding more sure than he felt.

Pauline sat back in relief. "If only Charles were here . . . What if I didn't have your family to turn to?"

Intent on moving the wagon to the opposite bank, Daniel concentrated on the task at hand, keeping his mouth shut. Besides, there wasn't anything he could say to Pauline about Charles that would make her feel better.

Jamie seemed delighted with their ride through the muddy river. "Doggies!" he shouted. "Doggies!"

Daniel was about to correct him when he realized that Jamie was right. Keeping pace with the wagon as they forded were Lad and Lass, who were enjoying a refreshing swim. Even Pauline forgot her anxiety for a moment and watched the dogs paddling along beside them.

One by one, the other wagons rolled into the river and started the slow journey across the muddy water. Daniel could hear the emigrants calling out to one another as they made the crossing behind him.

To calm Pauline, Daniel kept talking. "See, we're already a fourth of the way across," and later, "We've reached the halfway mark now."

Once, the oxen hesitated, the water rising above the wagon wheels, and he prodded them on with a sharp command and the crack of the whip. Finally, he announced gratefully, "We're almost there."

At last the dripping oxen stepped ashore, pulling the wagon clear of the river. When Daniel climbed down and led the team out of the way of oncoming wagons, Father came riding toward them, accompanied by Uncle Karl and Charles.

"Good work, Daniel," Father called out. "We'd hoped to be here sooner, but had some difficulties. Where are your mother and Aunt Pearl?"

"They're in the last wagons," he explained. "And please keep an eye on Ned when he has to swim the livestock across."

"Good idea," Father agreed, striking out into the river on his horse with Uncle Karl beside him. Charles spoke with Pauline for a moment, then followed the others into the muddy Platte.

Daniel was relieved when White Feather offered to line up the wagons. The man moved quickly and efficiently, and Daniel watched with interest as he directed the wagons to their places.

Looking back, Daniel noticed that the first few wagons had churned up the river bottom, which made the water deeper for those now coming through. He was troubled to see that the river reached all the way to the wagon beds as Mother and Aunt Pearl began their crossing. The going was rougher and slower, but at last all of the wagon train was safely across, followed by the loose livestock herded by Ned Taylor on horseback.

Ned grinned and waved at Daniel. "Made it just fine! No need for a rescue today!"

Later, Daniel told him that he had been praying for a safe crossing. "But I would have jumped in after you again if you'd needed me."

"I knew you would," Ned said. "Knew it all the time."

Behind them, Garth snorted. "You couldn't swim that far."

"With the Lord's help, I could," Daniel replied quietly.

Garth peered at him from under his dark brows, but didn't say another word.

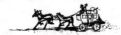

The trail began a slight rise as the covered wagons angled over to the North Fork of the Platte River. Now in mid-June, the countryside already looked dead and brown, except near the river. The oxen ate the dry grass without complaint, but the hard rutted ground pounded the wagon wheels mercilessly. Each evening, when they camped for the night, Daniel had to mend wagon wheels and hammer in wooden wedges to tighten the iron rims. And when one of the spare oxen died, its hide was cut into strips to tie up the worst of the wheels.

There were almost no trees to be found now, and even Suzannah gathered dried buffalo chips, for there was nothing else to burn for the cookfires.

"I thought you said you'd never collect buffalo chips!" Daniel called to her.

"I guess I can change my mind, can't I?" she retorted. But she wrinkled her nose in disgust as she picked up another and dropped it into her basket.

"Did you hear the song Mr. Murphy made up?" Daniel tried again, hoping to cheer her up.

She shook her head, and Daniel sang out, trying to imitate Mr. Murphy's Irish brogue:

It's fun to cook with buffalo chips
Take one that's newly born.
If I knew once what I know now,
I'd sailed around Cape Horn!

Even this chore became routine after a while, and Daniel wondered if a person could become used to almost anything on a long journey like this. Somehow, though, he could never get used to the sameness—same scenery, same beans and cornbread, same long, tiring days as the wagon wheels rolled round and round across the miles.

Then one day a new sight appeared on the horizon. "Mountains! The Rocky Mountains!" called Mordechai from far ahead on the trail. And as the news spread up and down the wagon train, others took up the cry: "The Rockies! Rocky Mountains ahead!"

Shielding his eyes with his hand, Daniel squinted into the fading sun. There they were—the Rockies—standing like a mighty gray fortress, their peaks jutting up against the red sky. And since the oxen were moving along well, he climbed up onto the driver's seat for a better look.

"First mountains since we crossed the Alleghenies nearly four months ago," Daniel reminded Pauline, who was sitting beside him now that Suzannah was dividing her time between Mother and Aunt Pearl.

"But the Rockies look newer and at least twice as high," Pauline said, taking out her sketchbook. "Sharp and jagged, not worn down like the Alleghenies." She made a few bold strokes on the page to capture the scene. Daniel knew she would fill in the details later.

As the days passed and they drew nearer, the Rocky Mountains loomed even larger and taller than at their first sighting. Since the country through which they were traveling still seemed quite flat, it appeared as if a giant hand had pushed up the earth in front of them. The mountains towered so high above the prairie that Daniel found himself tilting his head back to take in the whole majestic view.

As the trail led steadily upward, the weather also grew more changeable. "Storm's a'comin'," Mordechai warned one day.

"But there's only a small cloud in the sky," Daniel said.

"Keep yer eye on it."

The cloud moved toward them with amazing speed, growing larger and darker until the sky was black all around them. "Tie down yer belongin's!" Mordechai yelled. "Round up the livestock!"

Daniel shivered with the sudden drop in temperature and reached into his the wagon for his coat, then worked quickly to unhitch the oxen.

A flash of lightning zigzagged through the blackening sky, and the white canvas top shuddered noisily as the wind whistled across it. The lightning struck closer and closer, turning the darkness blue-white, and thunder clapped like cannons. Nearby, horses whinnied, their eyes rolling in terror. When the oxen were finally picketed in the corral, they strained at the stakes as if trying to break free. But the heavy chains held.

Daniel leapt into the wagon with Pauline and Jamie just as the rain began to pour. Soon it had soaked through the layers of canvas, and he put up the India rubber tent to keep them as dry as possible. But Jamie, who was already damp and cold, began to cry.

As the temperature continued to drop, the rain froze, becoming huge hailstones that pelted the livestock until they bawled in pain. With the rain inside and out and Jamie's constant crying, Pauline had had about all she could take. "What if it rains like this for days? We won't be able to cook or dry clothes . . . or even to move on. We'll be stuck!" she moaned.

Daniel looked out at the continuing downpour. "We're not really safe in these wagons, either. We're not close enough to the mountains yet for them to act as lightning rods. We could be struck—"

Pauline's face turned pale, and Daniel was angry with himself for not thinking before he spoke. Angry with Charles, too, for not being with his family. Most likely, Pauline's husband had climbed into one of the other wagons with the men, hoping to while away the time in a card game.

Hours later, the storm moved on, carrying its booming thunder and flashes of lightning toward the mountains. Daniel, like the others, was drenched. Worse, the canvas wagon coverings had been ripped in the storm and had to be mended.

"These things may never dry!" Pauline said as she wrung out their soggy clothes. "I haven't had on a clean dress in days."

Daniel tried to sympathize, but he was more concerned about the oxen. Since they had found little tender grass in the past few weeks, many of them were losing weight and growing weaker. But he wouldn't mention *that* to Pauline.

As the rain slackened, he climbed out of the wagon to check on the oxen and saw Charles slipping out of another wagon. Instead of coming to see about his wife and son, though, Charles was on his way to the corral.

The next morning, the oxen plodded through a sea of mud as they climbed the trail to higher, drier ground. And while no one had been hurt in the storm, within days many of the emigrants were sick with coughs and colds.

The days grew hotter and the nights even colder as they neared the mountains. At night, Daniel was glad to have Lad and Lass sleep in his small tent, but their warm bodies made it even harder to roll out in the morning.

It was on one of these cold mornings, as the wagons got underway, that Daniel again heard the sound of thunder. Worried, he looked up at the sky, but there was nothing but a bright blue canopy overhead.

"Buffalo!" shouted some emigrants up ahead. "Buffalo stampede!"

Daniel rushed to a nearby knoll that overlooked the plain they had just crossed. Thousands upon thousands of the dark beasts were running, churning up a great cloud of yellow dust with their hooves.

"They're comin' from the south . . . and we're in their path!" someone shouted. "We'll be trampled to death!"

Captain Monroe swung into action. "Unhitch those oxen! Chain 'em to the wagon wheels! Mordechai and the scouts will try to head the herd away from us!"

Daniel ran down from the knoll to help Suzannah and Mother with their oxen, while the buffalo thundered on.

"There's too many of them!" Suzannah cried. "The scouts will never be able to turn them!"

The earth shook under them, and the oxen bellowed, sensing the danger. Daniel's fingers fumbled with the hitches on Father's oxen. But finally he worked them loose and chained them to the wagon wheels.

"Look!" Mother screamed. "They're coming! God help us all!"

Help, Lord! Daniel prayed, too busy helping Pauline unhitch their oxen to look at the oncoming stampede. Leaving the yokes on, he pulled at the oxen. "Come on, Daisy and Marigold!" Daniel pleaded. "We're doing this for your own good!" But when he tugged on the oxen, they jerked away, stamped their hooves, and bawled with fright.

"I've never seen the team like this!" Pauline wailed. "They're usually so docile."

When they were at last secure, Daniel pushed Pauline toward the wagon, grabbed his father's spare rifle, and raced up on the knoll again. Men on horseback, including Father, Uncle Karl, and Charles, were already galloping toward the herd, trying desperately to turn the buffalo from the wagon train.

On and on came the huge herd. The men fired their rifles. As some of the buffalo crumpled and fell, the main herd slowly began to change direction. For an instant, it looked as if all would go well. Then, to his horror, Daniel saw twenty or more buffalo split off from the main herd and thunder directly toward them.

"Head 'em off, boys! Aim for the outside of the herd!" shouted Captain Monroe to Daniel and Garth.

Daniel aimed his rifle at the stampeding buffalo. The great beasts charged with their heads down, the wiry hair hanging over their eyes. As they ran toward the knoll where Daniel crouched, the bulls seemed to grow larger and larger, their massive humps rising like worn mountaintops. He shuddered at the gleam of white horns almost buried in the thick, shaggy manes.

"I'll take the first!" directed Captain Monroe. "Garth, you the second . . . Daniel, the third—"

Captain Monroe fired, and his buffalo veered into the herd, beginning to turn them before dropping to the ground. Garth shot at the second, and Daniel aimed at the third huge beast, then squeezed the trigger. To his amazement, his buffalo veered and fell, too.

"Keep shootin'!" called the captain.

Daniel reloaded and shot again, but this time, the animal thundered onward. The small herd passed the knoll

and, despite everything the boys could do, the great beasts struck the line of wagons, overturning several as they roared past.

Heart pounding, Daniel ran behind the rampaging buffalo toward his overturned wagon. A hen fluttered from a shattered coop as he approached.

"Pauline! Jamie!" Daniel called, dreading what he might find.

"Here," Pauline cried weakly. She stumbled out of the overturned wagon, Jamie screaming in her arms. "Where's Charles? I need Charles." She was shaking and her face was white.

Daniel saw that they weren't hurt. "I'll find him," he promised. "Wait here."

Daniel ran to his mother's overturned wagon. "Mother! Suzannah!"

"Are those animals gone?" his mother asked, sitting up amidst the jumble of furniture and dangling frying pans.

"They're not coming back?" Suzannah asked, untangling herself from a quilt and the upended mattress.

"They're gone," he assured them.

"What I wouldn't have given to have a rifle myself!" Suzannah said. "I'd have shot them right between the eyes when they came at us!"

"We saw them just before they crashed into our wagon," Mother explained. "Look here, where a hoof has cut the canvas! I thank the good Lord that buffalo didn't fall on top of us!"

Daniel interrupted. "Where's Charles? Pauline is pretty shook up—" Just then he saw Charles striding through the camp, brushing at his black suit. Pauline ran to him holding Jamie, and Charles, frowning, brushed them off. "Is the wagon damaged?" Daniel heard him ask.

Daniel turned away in disgust. Then he remembered: *Aunt Pearl!* "Be right back," he said, and set off at a run.

He found Aunt Pearl's wagon right side up, though damaged. Inside, she sat in her beloved rocker, holding the blue glass lamp her first husband had given her. There was a dazed expression on her face.

"Wasn't that a fright?" she said as he helped her out.

When Garth arrived, he cursed loudly at the buffalo and the damage they had caused. His crude language jolted Aunt Pearl right out of her shock.

"No matter what happens, you shouldn't talk like that, Garth," she said quietly.

"I'll cuss 'em all I want!" her stepson replied.

Just then Captain Monroe returned from his inspection of the other wagons. "Except for a few cuts and bruises, everyone's fine. It's a miracle . . . that's all I can say—a miracle that no one's badly hurt!"

Daniel nodded, still shaken. "It's a miracle all right."

Behind him, Garth said sarcastically, "That's not the only miracle. Daniel finally shot himself a real live buffalo. Good thing they weren't no hornets."

Daniel looked past Garth's taunting grin at the last of the buffalo disappearing over the horizon. *Sure, I shot a buffalo*, he thought. *But what will I have to do next to prove myself?*

CHAPTER EIGHT

For the rest of the day the wagon train was abuzz with stories about the buffalo. Thankfully, no one had been badly hurt, but there was plenty of work to be done. After they pulled up the overturned wagons, the men butchered the dead buffalo and gathered the scattered livestock. Meanwhile the women cooked buffalo strips for jerky on frames set up over the cookfires.

As Daniel helped Suzannah straighten up Pauline's wagon, he replayed the scene over and over in his mind. He could still see the huge herd coming toward them. He recalled aiming the rifle and squeezing the trigger, then seeing one of the great beasts fall to the ground. Slowly, a feeling of wonder and pride filled him. *Maybe I will be able to learn to hunt after all,* he thought.

When the family gathered for dinner, they were still

talking about the incident. "I don't think I'll ever forget those buffalo," Suzannah said. "I thought they'd run right over us!"

Father shook his head. "I thank God you're all still alive. When I saw those buffalo split away from the herd and stampede toward our wagons, I prayed like never before—" He broke off, too moved to finish.

"Prayer changes things," Mother said with confidence.

Aunt Pearl nodded. "Yes. It's prayer that saved us."

Garth's dark eyes snapped. "It didn't help my ma none!"

A silence hung between them before Aunt Pearl said kindly, "But she's in glory with the Lord now, Garth. I know you miss her, but she's in a better place. And all of her earthly worries are over."

"I don't hold much stock with that," he objected.

"Your father is trying to go on with his life," Aunt Pearl added. "And so am I, though it's not easy when you've lost loved ones. Only the Lord can help us through something like that."

Garth put his hands over his ears. "Don't go preachin' at me agin!" he said and stalked off.

Aunt Pearl sighed. "I do wish we could help him. I've prayed and prayed for him, for Karl, too, but they can't seem to forgive and forget."

Daniel's mother moved over to her side. "We'll pray with you for both of them, Pearl."

And right on the spot, Daniel did just that. *Heavenly Father,* he prayed silently, *give Uncle Karl and Garth Thy forgiveness for the Indian who killed Garth's mother. And let them open their hearts to Thy Holy Spirit so they can know Thou dost really hear and answer our prayers—*

Late in the afternoon, when Uncle Karl returned from helping Ned round up the livestock, he had bad news.

"Them buffalo not only stampeded the livestock, they run some of 'em to death. We got fewer spare oxen and cattle in the herd now." Then he looked at Aunt Pearl with a pained look in his eyes. "Your . . . milk cow is dead," he said, struggling to break the news to her.

Tears filled Aunt Pearl's eyes. "Poor old Elsa. We should have sold her in Independence."

Uncle Karl put an arm around Aunt Pearl's shoulder and patted her awkwardly. Daniel turned away, grateful to see that his new uncle cared enough to console Aunt Pearl about Elsa. Sometimes it seemed that Uncle Karl was softening, that he wasn't as mean and ornery as he was just blunt-spoken.

"Ned Taylor saved as much of the livestock as he could," Uncle Karl went on. "He's a hard worker, that feller."

"That he is," Father agreed. "For that matter, so are you and Garth. I've been meaning to thank both of you. The rest of us couldn't do what you're doing."

Uncle Karl gave a nod, color rising to his cheeks. "Better tend to my chores," he said, and left to inspect the damage to his wagon.

For supper, there was buffalo steak again, and plenty of meat to smoke for the journey ahead. "I suppose we'll be sick of it before long," said Daniel.

"Better than not eatin' at all," Uncle Karl said matter-of-factly.

Mordechai was up before dawn, shouting, "Catch up yer teams! Catch up!" And the day began before any of them were quite ready.

After breakfast, Captain Monroe called out the now familiar order, "Wagons, ho!"

As Daniel prodded his team forward down the trail, Charles rode past the line of wagons with a lofty wave to Pauline and Jamie. Daniel had half-expected him to mention the near disaster they'd been through. But Charles had accepted his family's deliverance as something that was due him, rather than something for which to be grateful.

As they rode on, the country grew more interesting. During their nooning stop, Pauline had some unusual rock formations to sketch—Courthouse and Jail Rocks. Captain Monroe stopped by to take a look at her sketches.

"A good likeness," he complimented her. "Before long, you'll have a whole day to sketch Chimney Rock."

"The names of the rocks sound like our street signposts back in Georgetown," Daniel remarked.

Captain Monroe laughed. "That's exactly what they are out here."

Charles rode up on Lucky with a scowl on his face. He didn't mind Pauline sketching, but he disliked her talking to other men, even older ones like the captain.

Captain Monroe saluted Charles and stepped back. "Mordechai wants us to double our guards, so there'll be four of us," he said, turning to Daniel. "You willing to stand guard duty for four hours with me tonight?"

Daniel was honored. "Yes, sir, I sure am."

"Bring your rifle then. The Sioux Indians around here are warrior horsemen. Likely they'll covet our horses."

Daniel nodded, feeling the old fears stirring as he was reminded of the dangers of guard duty.

"The Indians generally try to steal a few horses, then raise a loud whooping to frighten the others so they'll break loose and run," Captain Morris explained. "Once Indians get past the guards, they nearly always get away with some of the horses. Our job is to see that they don't."

That night Daniel sat alone outside the ring of wagons, his rifle half-cocked. In the light of the moon, the encampment was surprisingly bright. A wolf howled somewhere in the darkness beyond, and he shivered.

" 'I can do all things through Christ which strengtheneth me,' " he quoted from the Bible. "*All* things." He hoped that included fighting off wolves and savage Indians. The very thought kept him alert.

By the second hour, however, his eyelids were drooping. Then, thinking that the other guards would believe he was too young for guard duty if he couldn't stay awake, he forced himself to keep his eyes open.

Suddenly, he spotted something crawling through the grass in a nearby ravine. It looked like a wolf . . . a lone wolf . . . and yet there was something odd about its movements.

Quietly, Daniel rose and aimed the rifle. If the wolf came any closer—

At that moment, the "wolf" must have seen moonlight gleaming on the barrel of Daniel's rifle, for he rose up on his two feet and ran, bent over, in a zigzag direction.

"Indian!" Daniel yelled the alarm. "Indian! Over here!"

Shots rang out, but the Indian, disguised in a wolf skin, was already out of range.

Captain Monroe patted Daniel on the shoulder. "Good job. I've heard of a wolf in sheep's clothing, but not an Indian in wolf's clothing!"

"But I almost fell asleep," Daniel admitted truthfully.

"Not easy to stay awake in the middle of the night," the captain answered. "I have trouble sometimes myself."

His words lifted Daniel's spirits.

On and on they traveled, seeing the fantastical Chimney Rock for a full day's journey, just as the captain had promised. It looked like a giant funnel set upside down on the land.

The line of rust-colored formations continued toward Scott's Bluff, which resembled an old castle. While the wagon train was camped nearby, the first baby of the trip was born and named "Matthew Scott Brady" in honor of the bluff.

At the end of June, the emigrants sighted snow-capped Laramie Peak bristling up on the horizon, then Fort Laramie far ahead. To Daniel, the fort, with its high walls and guard towers at the huge gates, looked strong and safe.

"It might look like a fort," Captain Monroe said, "but it's actually a trading post where we can buy supplies."

Mordechai, who had just ridden in from scouting the fort, let out a snort of disgust. "Them traders charge ten times what anythin's worth," he warned.

As they rode closer, however, Daniel could see at least a hundred buffalo-skin tepees surrounding the fort. "Look at all the Indians!"

"What if they're gettin' up a war party?" Uncle Karl asked. "They could chew up this whole wagon train in no time a'tall."

"Ain't likely," Mordechai said. "They're Sioux. The warriors are ridin' ponies—"

Garth interrupted, "Yeah, but they're carryin' lances and bows and arrows. Ain't that proof enough?"

Mordechai shook his head. "They got their women and children with 'em. They're tradin', but hold onto yer belongin's, 'specially your guns, since they figger we're where we don't belong. Just so's they don't git anxious, we'll make camp in the open."

They circled their wagons tightly, within sight of the fort and Indian encampment. But before they were completely settled, Charles rode out toward the fort on Lucky.

"Charles, please don't leave," Pauline begged.

He shot her an angry look and rode on.

Captain Monroe folded his arms. "If he's a gambler, those traders will beat him out of everything he owns, even his horse."

When the Indians rode over for trading some time later, they brought moccasins and skins with them. Their shining black eyes took in everything in the emigrant camp, as if they were making mental notes of the layout. It gave Daniel a funny feeling.

"Break out yer tradin' goods if you see anythin' you want," Mordechai said.

To Daniel's amazement, Mother, Pauline, and Aunt Pearl all traded beads for moccasins. "They've been wanting some like mine ever since I got these back on the trail," Suzannah explained. "I may never wear high-topped shoes again!"

Daniel shook his head. "I'm not too surprised at you, but I never thought I'd see Mother wearing Indian moccasins!"

Overhearing him, his mother laughed. "I might surprise you even more. I'm so tired of my calico and gingham frocks that I've been thinking about trading for one of those beaded deerskin dresses."

"Mother!" Daniel exclaimed. When she laughed, he was relieved to see that she hadn't been serious.

The Indians left at last, and some of the men made wagon repairs, while others rode in to Fort Laramie to stock up on flour, rice, beans, and other supplies. Even more important, Daniel thought, the oxen were resting and grazing on decent grass.

As they finished supper, Father announced, "We've marked off more than five hundred miles now. Just the first stage of our journey."

"That's all?" Daniel asked.

Father nodded. "Afraid so. We've still got a long way to go."

At that moment, Charles galloped into camp, a dozen or more Indians riding hard on his heels. Pauline gasped as he jumped Lucky over a gap between the wagons.

"What's wrong, man?" Captain Monroe called. "Why are those Indians chasing you?"

"They're after Lucky!"

Mordechai stepped up and blocked the gap, pointing his rifle in the direction of the Indians and speaking to them in Sioux. He listened as they answered.

Finally he nodded and turned to Charles. "They say you cheated 'em at cards . . . that you owe 'em yer hoss."

Charles dismounted, flinging his reins to Daniel. "I wouldn't gamble with Indians—"

Mordechai scratched his head and squinted, giving him a long look. "*They* say you *did*."

"Then they're speaking for the traders," Charles said. "I don't owe anyone Lucky. Anyhow, I *won*."

Mordechai spoke with the Indians again. At last he put down his rifle. "I've convinced 'em thet there's a misunderstandin'. But the only way they're willin' to settle it and let our wagon train pass on tomorrow is fer us to make breakfast fer all of 'em. Seems they cotton to the white man's beans and cornbread."

Mother was shocked. "But there are hundreds of them!"

Mordechai went on. "Herrington, you caused this with yer gamblin', so you'll have to pay fer the supplies fer the feast. Either that, or there's goin' to be trouble gettin' past 'em tomorrow. They're dead set on it."

Both emigrants and Indians stared angrily at Charles. Finally, he dug into his pocket and produced a coin pouch. "Take it!" He flung the leather pouch to the ground.

Daniel picked up the pouch and handed it to Mordechai. Opening it, the old scout nodded, then drew up the strings while the Indians waited in silence. Satisfied, they rode off.

Charles was furious. "They're liars! And you're taking their word!"

"Don't matter who's lyin', you put all of us in danger by gamblin' and then ridin' in alone like thet," Mordechai answered. "You give 'em an excuse ta make this demand. You think it's costin' yer winnin's, but I tell you thet ev'ry woman in this camp will end up payin' in hard labor afore we're done. It's them has to do all the cookin'. I got half a mind to make you put on an apron yerself."

Charles shot him a murderous look, then climbed into his wagon, no doubt to put an end to the lecture.

After a while, Mordechai and White Feather rode back to the fort to buy extra supplies for the Indians' breakfast. In the meantime, the men found Charles sulking in his wagon and made him help them dig the pits in the ground where the beans would cook all night.

When Mordechai and White Feather returned with the sacks of supplies slung over their horses, they found the pit fires started. "Be sure them beans is well cooked," he ordered. "We don't want them Injuns claimin' we give 'em belly aches!"

The women were still not certain how to go about making cornbread enough for the huge camp of Indians. "We'll have to begin making cornbread tonight, then keep at it in the morning," Mother suggested.

"They'll be waitin' come first light with their buffalo skins spread out fer tablecloths," Mordechai said.

The next morning Pauline's wagon was emptied of all its crates, barrels, quilts, and clothing to carry the breakfast feast to the Indians.

"You stay right here and try to keep out of trouble," Mordechai ordered Charles. "Now, who volunteers to take the food over and serve the Injuns?"

Pauline handed Jamie to Aunt Pearl. "I'll go," she offered.

Mother and Father joined Pauline, then Suzannah. Daniel couldn't help remembering his father's oft-spoken words: *For better or for worse, this family stays together. We won't let the circle be broken.* Then Daniel, too, stepped forward.

"Garth and I'll stay with Charles and the wagons," Uncle Karl offered. "Somebody's got to keep an eye on 'em." He cast a suspicious eye at Pauline's husband.

No one spoke as they walked through the circle of wagons toward the Indian encampment until the last moment, when Mordechai said, "Guard yer pots and pans well, or it'll be the last you'll see of 'em."

The Indians sat down on their buffalo skins, their empty bowls in front of them, their dark eyes watching the emigrants' every move. Daniel grabbed a pot of beans and a ladle and began to fill the Indians' wooden bowls. He smiled as kindly as he could at the Indians around him, but received only solemn stares in return.

Beside him, Suzannah passed out pieces of cornbread. "Hope you enjoy them," she said in her most pleasant voice.

Serving so many people was hard work, and his own stomach churned with hunger. "We won't have enough for our own breakfasts," he told Mordechai.

"Can't be helped," the old scout said. "Jest keep on dishin' out the food as far as it'll go. Cap'n Monroe and the others are readyin' the wagon train so's we kin make tracks as soon as we return."

When all of the beans and salt pork were gone, Daniel showed his empty pot to the Indians. "That's all. There isn't any more."

Some of them began to object, but Mordechai reasoned with them. At last, he said, "Let's get movin'! Them Injuns say they're still hungry!"

By the time they had returned to their camp with their empty pots and pans, Daniel saw that Uncle Karl and Garth had already turned Pauline's wagon, ready to make a fast exit.

"What a sight we must make," Suzannah said. "I wouldn't be surprised if those Indians are laughing behind our backs."

In spite of himself, Daniel had to grin. "I guess it does look like we're retreating. Probably what they had in mind."

Mother agreed. "It's something else to remember— the day we fed hundreds of Sioux Indians beans and cornbread for breakfast! Our friends in Georgetown will never believe it!"

"Nor mine in Missouri!" said Aunt Pearl.

"What next?" Daniel asked. "What next?"

CHAPTER NINE

The Indians sat cross-legged on their blankets, as still as statues, watching the first few wagons pass. As his oxen plodded nearer toward their encampment, Daniel wondered what they would do.

Beside him, Suzannah was jittery, too. "If only old Marigold and the others could move faster!"

"Just what I was thinking. But maybe it's best if we don't seem to be in a hurry."

When Captain Monroe rode by on his horse, Daniel asked, "You think they'll come after us?"

The captain tugged on his beard as if he had been asking himself the same question. "I doubt it. They probably figure they got the best of us already. And, as Mordechai said, they have their women and children along."

Daniel's oxen lumbered slowly along the trail, the creak of the wagon wheels seeming louder than ever. For a long moment, they drew even with the staring Indians, and he risked a glance in their direction. They didn't budge. Not a muscle. Not an eyelid.

Suddenly he remembered reading that Indians prided themselves on never showing emotion—pain, joy, and especially fear—and that they valued the same ability in others. Right now, Daniel's heart was hammering so hard he felt sure they could see it jumping in his chest. But he was determined not to let them see how scared he was. Lifting his chin, he looked straight ahead and strolled past the Indians as if he had all of the time in the world.

"Whew!" Suzannah said when they were well down the trail.

Captain Monroe let out a deep breath himself, and even his horse snorted. "I expect they won't bother us anymore, but I'll feel better when we leave Fort Laramie far in our dust."

Leaning over, Daniel spoke to the captain quietly, so Pauline couldn't hear. "I'm really sorry about Charles causing the trouble."

Captain Monroe waved aside his apology. "You had nothing to do with it. In fact, you helped feed the Indians, didn't you?"

"But Charles is part of our family," Daniel explained.

"There's someone like Herrington in most families," the captain said. "At least all of you stick together."

"It's not always easy," Suzannah put in. "But Uncle Franklin says a family should *try* to stay together."

"That the circle shouldn't be broken," Daniel added.

"Good advice," said the captain. They traveled in silence for a while until the captain spoke again. "According to Mordechai, we have a greater trial ahead . . . the North Fork of the Platte is too deep to ford. It's another situation needing prayer." And with that, he dug in his heels and wheeled his horse off toward the rear of the wagon train.

Soon the trail grew rougher, and they could no longer travel along the river. Instead, they drove the wagons up and down the blackish hills. It was still Sioux Indian country, and the next time Mordechai rode in, he warned, "Be on yer guard. If they come out tradin', make a good show of yer firearms."

When a party of Sioux approached, Daniel got out his rifle, though it was unloaded. Two wagons ahead, Garth also made a "good show" of his rifle, and Daniel was sure it was loaded. *Lord, please don't let Garth shoot,* Daniel prayed. *And keep Charles from making more trouble.*

"Indians!" Jamie yelled gleefully from the wagon. "Indians!"

Daniel jumped, ready to cover Jamie's mouth before he offended the visitors. But the Indian women pointed and smiled at the child, who waved at them. It was the first time Daniel had seen an Indian smile. Garth, however, continued to glower at them from under his dark brows, his rifle in hand.

Captain Monroe's "Wagons, ho!" was more than welcome this time, and they moved on down the trail.

Ten hard days of travel later, they came to the part of the Platte River they had been dreading—the North Fork.

"Well, look at that!" said Captain Monroe in amazement. "Seems our prayers have been answered. Someone's left a ferryboat behind for us. Maybe the crossing won't be so bad, after all."

"Hurrah!" some of the emigrants called out.

But Daniel eyed the raftlike ferry with concern. Like

the ferry at the Kansas River, it was built of logs that had been tied together with leather thongs, and there were strips of buffalo hide for pulling loads across.

"It'll help," he told Suzannah, "but it's still going to be hard work swimming the livestock across."

"And you've got to keep an eye on Ned," Suzannah warned, half in jest.

Daniel nodded thoughtfully. "Maybe I can trade places with him. He can load the wagons on the ferry, and I'll help swim the livestock."

Ned was glad to trade. "You know I'm not partial to rivers . . . 'cept for drinkin'," he joked.

Daniel grinned. He and Ned had become friends even though the farm boy was older. He was a fine fellow, which made it all the harder to understand why his family had let him go so far away.

The crossing took hours, but at last all of the wagons and livestock were safely across, and the emigrants could settle down to their nooning and a well-deserved rest.

When they set out again, Suzannah felt little sad. "Goodbye, Platte River. We'll be keeping company with the Sweetwater now."

"It's like losing an old friend," Daniel said. "But we're finally entering the heart of the West."

June passed into July, and the grass wasn't as plentiful. Dust billowed up around them as they traveled across the scorched land. In one day they lost two oxen to hunger and another to heat stroke.

Then a man died of fever, leaving his wife and three children to mourn, followed by the French lady, Mrs. Poisot. This gave Daniel plenty to worry about. What if Mother and Father died of the fever? What if he himself got sick? *Lord, don't let us die . . . not here . . . not now!* And to his immense relief, no one else contracted the sickness.

A steep canyon forced them to take a route farther from the river and green grass for a week. "And it won't be the last time," Mordechai warned. "You'd best git used to harder goin'."

"You mean, harder than it's been?" Daniel asked. Mordechai nodded. "You ain't seen nothin' yet!"

"Boom! Boom!"

Daniel awakened to the sound of gunfire. Alarmed, he rolled out from under the wagon and into the safety of the circle of wagons.

"Happy Fourth of July!" shouted the emigrants to one another. "Happy Fourth of July!"

Suzannah laughed at him. "You sure looked scared. Did you think we were being attacked by wild Indians?"

Daniel felt his face redden.

"Daniel, you're so red-faced, you look like an Indian," Suzannah teased. "Anyway, today's the day we reach Independence Rock, remember?"

Daniel recalled that the travelers had been urged to arrive at Independence Rock no later than the Fourth of July, or they could be caught in the mountain blizzards later. "Guess that means we'll be there in time," he said.

After breakfast, he hitched up the oxen, talking to them as usual. "Good work, boys. We're on time. Keep it up now."

They rolled their eyes. They were all thinner, and he hoped there would be good grass and water for them ahead. Just for the fun of it, he tickled Marigold under the chin. "No water or grass again today, boy," he told the ox. "But tonight we'll make camp at Independence Rock."

They trudged on through the dry canyons, and finally the famous landmark came into sight, with the Sweetwater River flowing below.

"Independence Rock!" announced Daniel, whose wagon was now first in line.

"It looks like a big gray whale stranded in the valley," Suzannah observed.

"More like a turtle to me," Daniel said. "But I aim to get my name on it with those of the mountain men and other pioneers. I might not be a 'Bible-totin' Jedediah Smith,' but we've come this far, and I intend to announce it to the world!"

At the sight of Independence Rock, the spirits of almost everyone in the wagon train lifted considerably. Mordechai and Captain Monroe, however, were worried about the pools of alkali water all around.

"They're poison to the animals," Mordechai said. "Keep 'em away from thet water."

"I'll take care of the animals," Father told Daniel. "Why don't you and Suzannah go up and inscribe our names on the rock?"

"Can we take Ned, too?" Daniel asked. "He's worked mighty hard with the livestock."

"I'll ask the captain," Father replied. "Meanwhile, you can mix grease and gunpowder to paint our names for posterity."

Soon after, Ned arrived with a grin on his face. "I'm much obliged to your father for gettin' me some time off."

"Come on then," Daniel said. "Let's climb up that rock and make our mark in the world."

They started up the rugged base of the rock together, then Daniel took the lead, Suzannah and Ned trailing behind. Here and there were names of others who had passed this way. Nearby, someone had carved: "The Oregon Company arrived July 26, 1843."

"Maybe we'll see them when we get to Oregon," Daniel said. Then as they climbed on, he added, "I plan to carve my whole name in honor of Captain Lewis, even if it's more work. Besides, 'Meriwether' and 'Oregon' sound just right together."

Jack Murphy, whose large family was headed for California, was just ahead of them. "I'm writin', 'Jack Murphy, future Californian,'" he announced.

"Can't see why you're heading for a place so empty of Americans," called Daniel. "But everyone to his own opinion."

Jack Murphy laughed and climbed on.

Arriving near the top of the incline, they found a flat surface for carving, and Daniel took out his jackknife. "Let's say, 'Captain Monroe's Oregon Party of 1848' because there are others. Then we can carve our own names and paint over the whole thing so it's readable for some time to come."

"Just don't carve *my* name," Suzannah warned. "I want to do it myself."

Daniel gave a laugh. "Don't you think I know better than to carve it for you?"

She grinned. "I wasn't sure." Then she scampered to a far corner of the rock to begin carving her name.

When Suzannah was out of earshot, Ned smiled at their banter. "I wish I'd come from a family where . . . folks got along like yours."

"Ours isn't so perfect," Daniel said as he began to carve. "But most of us get along most of the time."

Ned took out his own jackknife. "Our family sure didn't," he said, hesitating as if unsure whether to go on. "My pa . . . well, he drank a lot . . . and he beat Ma . . . and the rest of us. Even the little 'uns."

Shocked, Daniel looked up. "I didn't know that, Ned. I'm really sorry."

Ned nodded, his brow furrowed. After a moment he asked, "What makes your family so different?"

"I guess what holds us together," Daniel said, bending over his carving, "is that most of us know God planned it that way. Christ said we're to love one another . . . but not just the ones in our family . . . others, too."

"But how can you love someone who beats you?"

"That sure would be hard." Daniel sat back on his heels and gave Ned a sympathetic look. "But God's people are supposed to forgive, even the ones who hurt us."

"But how?" Ned asked.

"It's not easy," Daniel admitted. "First, you have to say 'I forgive you,' whether you feel like it or not. Then, if you don't have any love for the person, you ask God to give you some of His. If you hold fast on that, over and over, you'd be surprised how it works out."

There was a look of wonder on Ned's face. "I never heard anything like that before."

"It's what I have to do with Charles and Garth all the time." They carved on quietly for a while, then Daniel asked, "Didn't your folks ever take you to church?"

"Never did. Guess they was too ashamed of our clothes or somethin'. I . . . I hope you won't tell any of the other folks. I never talked to anyone 'bout this before."

"You have my word," Daniel promised. "I won't even tell Suzannah unless you say so." He carved on, wishing he knew how to help Ned, for he sounded so full of hurt. "I guess you were glad to leave for Oregon then."

"Mostly," Ned replied, "except for leavin' my little brother and sister. The older ones were gettin' as mean and ornery as Pa."

"You don't have to be like your Pa," Daniel said, still carving. "You can follow Christ instead."

"I sure do wish you'd tell me how to do that."

Daniel paused in his carving. "Why, you just say something like this: 'Heavenly Father, I know I need You because I can't even love or forgive by myself. I'm sorry, and I want You to change me. Send Your Son, Jesus Christ, to save me from my sins—"

To Daniel's amazement, Ned bowed his head and began to repeat Daniel's words. It all happened so quickly that Daniel almost dropped his jackknife. When they finished the prayer, Ned lifted his head. His eyes were shining.

"Now you're a Christian, Ned!" Daniel said. "You're a brother in the Lord to me and Suzannah, too. You've got a spiritual family now that's even closer than your own blood family at home."

Ned beamed with pleasure. And Suzannah, who had overheard the last part of his prayer, rushed over to give him a big hug.

"You can always remember the day you accepted

Christ as your Savior," Daniel told Ned. "July 4, 1848, on Independence Rock."

"That reminds me," Ned said. "There's something else I'd like to do." He took out his jackknife again.

When he came back, they sat for a few minutes in the warm sunshine, looking out over the scene below. In the clear air, every detail seemed as if it had been carved clean and sharp—the circle of wagons, smoke rising from the cookfires, the Rocky Mountains with their high peaks to the West, and behind them in the distance, another wagon train making its way up the trail.

"You may not be Bible-totin' Jedediah Smith, Daniel, but I guess he'd be mighty proud of you right now," Suzannah told him.

Daniel scarcely heard her words. "You know," he remarked, "I've been thinking that even Jedediah Smith is our brother, and someday in Glory we may be able to tell him about Ned's conversion right here on Independence Rock."

When they were ready to climb back down to the camp, they looked once more at the words they had carved: "Captain Monroe's Oregon Party of 1848. Daniel Meriwether Colton. Suzannah Colton . . ." Reading the final inscription, Daniel grinned. Ned had written: "Ned Taylor, *Christian*."

The next day the wagon train followed the Sweetwater River into the Rocky Mountains. And by the next afternoon, they had reached the banks of the river where the emigrants made camp. For the first time in weeks the women were able to do their washing, and soon they were spreading the clean wet clothes on the rocks and shrubs to dry.

With an afternoon free, Daniel decided to try out the new fishhooks Suzannah had given him for his birthday. He and Ned found a quiet place downriver, settled on a big rock under the trees, and threw their fishing lines into the clear mountain stream. There was no sound except for the twitter of birds and the sighing of the breeze in the tops of the cottonwood trees.

After a while Ned broke the peaceful silence. "Reverend Benjamin wants to baptize me tomorrow, right here in the Sweetwater River. He thinks it's just as good as bein' baptized in a church."

Daniel looked up at the trees and the high peaks and ridges beyond. "Can't think of a better place for it myself."

"Ain't no words to ever thank you for savin' my life," Ned said. "I'm truly glad to have you for a friend." At that moment he felt a tug on his fishing pole, gave it a jerk, and hauled up a good-sized mountain trout. The silvery body thrashed the clear water before Ned, grinning from ear to ear, landed the fish on the bank.

When they had settled down once more, Daniel took up the conversation. "Just don't expect me to be perfect," he warned Ned. "You've got to follow Christ, not me or anyone else. I've got troubles myself." *Like not always loving Charles and Garth and Uncle Karl,* he reminded himself. *And having to ask God to help me forgive them over and over again.*

"Expect there's a lot to learn about bein' a Christian," Ned replied.

"More than you know," said Daniel. "It seems that God has worked it out so there's no end to the learning as long as we're here on earth."

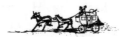

The next morning, Mordechai stood in the center of the half-circle of wagons facing the river. "There's raidin'

Crow to the north, and Blackfoot and Snake war parties to the west. Are you sure you want to stop fer a Sabbath service?"

"What you've just told us makes it all the more important," replied Reverend Benjamin.

Mordechai posted guards in the forest and along the rocks around the encampment. As usual, Garth, Charles, and Uncle Karl volunteered for guard duty.

"They're just trying to get out of attending the service," Suzannah said.

"That's because they don't know what they're missing!" Daniel answered.

At the riverside, they found that Reverend Benjamin had set up the large wooden cross he had brought all the way from Independence, Missouri. When the emigrants were settled, they started the service with a song:

This is the day the Lord hath made;
He calls the hours His own:
Let Heaven rejoice, let earth be glad,
And praise surround the throne.

Daniel glanced at Ned as they sang out. Ned didn't know the words, but his face glowed with happiness. Yesterday he had shared his mountaintop experience with the pastor, and later the Reverend Benjamin had told Daniel, "The Lord used you well with Ned Taylor, son."

"It all happened so fast—"

The gray-haired man had nodded in understanding. "That's often true when the Holy Spirit has already softened someone's heart as He had Ned's. Captain Monroe, your father, and I have been praying for Ned since the day we hired him."

Now Daniel listened to the worship service with interest. Reverend Benjamin spoke about the woodland

and prairies through which they had passed, and of the mountains yet ahead. "In a sense, it's like the wilderness where Moses and the children of Israel wandered," he said.

Daniel could really sympathize with those early travelers who had left Egypt so long ago and followed Moses to their new home far away.

"For most of us," Reverend Benjamin continued, "there will be wilderness times ... difficult times ... ahead, too. Through all of these, we must honor and even praise God. We must ask Him to change our sinful natures and to make us holy vessels for His use."

The pastor's gaze rested on Daniel for an instant, then moved on to Ned. "One of us was used recently to lead another in this party to the Lord Jesus. So it is my privilege this morning to baptize Ned Taylor as a symbol of his new life in Christ. If any others here have felt the gentle call of our Savior and wish to present themselves for baptism, they may come forward at this time."

Daniel found himself hoping that, by some miracle, Charles or Garth or Uncle Karl might suddenly show up from guard duty, or that someone else might step forward, but no one made a move except Ned. Nonetheless, Daniel thought it the most beautiful church service he'd ever seen, with the forest and mountains framed against the sky like a green cathedral.

Daniel watched with a lump in his throat as Ned was baptized in the Sweetwater River while the congregation sang softly. And when the Reverend Benjamin lifted Ned, wet from the river, his face shining with joy, the melody of the beautiful hymn lingered in the mountain air:

Amazing grace, how sweet the sound,
That saved a wretch like me,

I once was lost, but now am found,
Was blind, but now I see—

Feeling a presence behind him, Daniel turned to find Mordechai, his ancient hat in his hand. With his white hair blowing in the breeze, the old scout looked like a prophet of old in Bible pictures.

The joyous sounds of the music followed Daniel long after the service had ended, and Ned's smile didn't fade for the rest of the day. For the life of him, Daniel couldn't understand why anyone could choose to keep a heart filled with bitterness and revenge when that person could have peace and freedom. He wondered if Garth and Uncle Karl and Charles would ever know that peace.

In the evening after supper, Reverend Benjamin asked Daniel to join him for a walk by the river. When they had run out of talk about the mountains and the long journey, the pastor paused. "Son, have you ever felt the Lord calling you to be His man, His minister?"

Daniel's mouth dropped open. "No . . . no, sir. I guess I haven't—"

"Well, young man, I think you should pray about it."

From a distance, the Rockies had seemed a great gray wall, but Mordechai knew the Sweetwater River route well. Now the wagon train wound through the valley before it climbed higher and higher into the trees.

As the days passed, the climb became more and more difficult. Some days there was neither trail nor track, only huge splits in the earth. Daniel helped the others dig rock and dirt clods to fill the gullies so they could drive the oxen and wagons across.

"You've been awfully quiet lately, Daniel," Suzannah said, walking alongside him again.

He knew he hadn't been much of a traveling companion, but how could he tell her that he had been praying about what God might want him to do with his life? Suzannah was a believer, but Daniel didn't know whether she'd understand this next step he wanted to take, and he wasn't ready to discuss it with anyone. The fact was, he hadn't gotten an answer to his prayers yet, so he just shrugged.

He breathed in the sweet smell of wildflowers. Everything about them was lush and green here at this level, and willow groves gave shade for their noonings. But as they climbed even higher, the air grew so cool that the women brought out blankets against the cold.

"Mountain goats!" Suzannah shouted one day, pointing to a strange sight.

"Sure enough," Daniel replied, amazed to see the nimble animals jumping from cliff to cliff. It seemed a little like his own spiritual journey. He had climbed and climbed over difficult ground, but once in a while, he reached a high place in his walk with the Lord. Then he, too, felt like leaping about like the frisky goats and praising God for all He had done. Daniel was sure it would be like that again when he discovered just what God had planned for him.

The next day Captain Monroe rode down the column of wagons, stopping to pass on welcome news. "We're nearing South Pass," he told them.

"Will it be a hard climb?" Daniel asked about the famous mountain crossing through the Rockies.

The captain only smiled mysteriously. "You'll see."

To Daniel's surprise, South Pass was like a broad plain. The opening yawned nearly twenty miles wide between two walls of solid mountains.

At the Pass, the wagons came to a halt. "Isn't this

something?" Daniel asked Suzannah. "I thought we'd be teetering from dangerous ridges—"

"And hanging on by our fingernails!" Suzannah added, looking about. "Where's the dividing place, where the water begins to flow toward the Pacific Ocean instead of toward the Atlantic?"

Daniel didn't know, so they asked the captain.

"Mordechai says no one is certain," Captain Monroe replied.

Daniel was dumbfounded. "You mean we're at the great pass of the Rocky Mountains, and no one knows exactly where the highest place is?"

Captain Monroe laughed. "Not even Mordechai or our scout, so they say."

It took them only a day to cross the easy slope, stopping halfway to marvel at snow in August.

Daniel made a ball of snow and hurled it at Suzannah. "Got you!"

"Oh no, you don't!" she replied, ducking as the snowball spattered harmlessly against the mountain boulder behind her. Grabbing a handful of snow, she ran toward him. "Just for that, Daniel Meriwether Colton, you're going to get snow down your neck!"

He ran, but to his surprise, Pauline grabbed him from behind and held him down while Suzannah managed to cram some of the icy stuff down the inside of his collar. He struggled, laughing. Suddenly the grin faded. Maybe playing in the snow like this wasn't fitting for a boy who was thinking about becoming a minister. But when he looked, there was the dignified Reverend Benjamin, cocking his arm to aim a snowball in Father's direction! He guessed the Lord didn't mind a little good-natured fun.

The next morning, when Daniel skimmed ice from the top of the water buckets, Mordechai's grim warning came to mind: "We'll have to move on fast through them mountains, lest we be snowed in." Maybe for the first time, Daniel realized his prediction could come true. He lost no time in readying the oxen to move on.

Pointing out a gap in the mountains to Pauline that morning, Daniel made a prediction of his own. "See that spot over there? We'll likely be there by noon."

Instead, it took two days of hard travel to reach it, for the air was so clear that everything seemed nearer than it actually was. As Mordechai explained, "We kin see twenty, thirty mile across these valleys. A heap faster than we kin travel."

It was hard enough going uphill with the oxen and the cumbersome wagons, but harder still to keep them from running away down the steep grades. Worst of all, that very day one of the Murphys' wagons went over a cliff and crashed down the mountainside.

Daniel caught his breath as he peered over the ledge at the wreckage far below. "Good thing no one was inside," he told his father, feeling the old fear churning in the pit of his stomach.

"Better give the Murphys our extra buffalo blanket and whatever else we can spare," Father said when Mother asked what she could do. "They'll never make it without some help."

"But they're all safe and sound. It's best to count our blessings at a time like this," said Mother as she hurried to gather up some things to take over to their friends.

Daniel wished he hadn't seen the splintered wagon and poor crumpled oxen lying on the rocks. It wouldn't be an easy sight to put out of mind. What if his wagon went over with Pauline and Jamie inside? And why didn't Charles take over anyway? It was his rightful responsibility as the head of his family.

Daniel trudged on beside the oxen, his thoughts heavy and dark. Dangers lurked around every turn in the trail. As if that weren't bad enough, there were always the endless aggravations with Garth, Charles, and Uncle Karl.

He could be grateful, at least, that they hadn't seen any more Indians. But when was he ever going to feel like a real frontiersman?

CHAPTER
TEN

Ever since South Pass, they had been traveling downhill. Now Mordechai rode by on No-Name and pointed out a trail through the trees. "That there's the old road to Fort Bridger," he told them. "But we're takin' the cut-off."

"Is it safe?" Daniel's father asked.

"Safe as anythin' else hereabouts," said the old guide. "Only a mite more'n a hunderd mile to Bear River. But first, we'll rest fer a day at Big Sandy to feed and water the livestock. After thet, it's forty mile of bad desert. May as well turn what's left of yer hens into chicken soup now."

"Why?" Daniel asked.

"They won't make it through the desert," Mordechai replied. "Ain't no water, no grass . . . nothin' till Green River.'"

"Good thing we didn't name the hens like we did the oxen,"Daniel told Suzannah.

She nodded, her braids bobbing on her shoulders.

That night Daniel choked down stewed chicken for supper. Glancing around at the others, he saw that they weren't objecting at all, but seemed to enjoy the meal. Fine frontiersman *he* was. Of course, the others hadn't slept under the wagon and become so well acquainted with the hens.

At Big Sandy River, Daniel helped the men cut and load grass to take along in the wagons for the livestock. Meanwhile, Suzannah and the women filled up all of the jugs and kegs with water to last them through the desert.

"Wagons, ho-o!" shouted Captain Monroe, waving his hat westward. "Wagons, ho-o!"

An hour later, Daniel and Suzannah gazed out across the countryside ahead. For as far as they could see, it was flat and barren, with only a few clumps of dried sagebrush and rocks.

"It looks so . . . so empty," Daniel said in dismay.

"I've never seen anything like it in my whole life," Suzannah said, her eyes wide.

Pauline sketched the sight from her seat in the wagon as the oxen plodded onward. "It's beautiful in a way, though," she said. "A strange, fearsome kind of beauty."

"Fearsome" was the word for it, Daniel thought. It was a harsh land. Bright sunshine reflected off the sand, turning the ground and even the sky a gritty yellow.

The wagon train traveled across the desert in a straggly line to avoid the clouds of dust kicked up by the other wagons. They bumped through ravines and white alkali ponds glistening a deathly white in the sun. Soon Daniel's eyes, nose, and mouth were filled with dust. And the clumps of sagebrush tore at the oxen's legs and undersides, choking the wagons' progress.

Every hour or so, Daniel grabbed the ax and chopped the sagebrush away from his oxen. It scratched his arms and snagged his trouser legs. "Doing my best for you," he told them, feeling faint in the blazing sun.

Mordechai called for extra watering stops, but there were only a few swallows of water for each of the oxen. Worse, a ghastly mirage of a lake gleamed on the horizon, always just ahead.

"Marigold looks sickly," Suzannah said. "Do you suppose he was weak from the beginning? Maybe that's why he lay down on the first day out—"

Daniel didn't want to think about the possibility of losing Marigold. "Keep your mind on the green forests and the rivers in Oregon."

"And catching salmon," she added.

In the afternoon, the exhausted oxen pulled the wagons straight into the desert sun. Blinded by its brightness, Daniel saw the land and the sky as a shimmering yellow blur before his eyes.

"Look—" Suzannah pointed out the carcasses of dead animals littering the trail.

To make it worse, here and there the wagons passed furniture that earlier wagon trains had thrown out to lighten their loads—trunks, old bureaus, and even a heavy printing press.

"Keep your mind on God and Oregon," Daniel reminded her.

That night in the desert, Captain Monroe said, "We made nineteen miles today. Wish it'd been more."

Then Daniel's mother asked, "What do we use to start the cookfires? There's no wood or buffalo chips . . . only sagebrush."

Aunt Pearl shook her head. "Believe it or not, I'd welcome cooking over buffalo chips again."

"And I wouldn't even mind gathering them up," Suzannah said.

Daniel wished he could help them. But there was other work for him to do. He allowed the oxen their few swallows of water, then made some repairs to the wagon. In the heat of the desert, the wheels and wagon tongues and even the wagon beds had shrunk.

The next morning, his two lead oxen, Lily and Petunia, were so weak that they had to be left behind. "Best to shoot 'em," Mordechai told Charles.

"Then I'll do it," Charles said. "Better than their being killed by wolves."

Daniel turned away as Charles pointed his rifle. Two shots tore through the air. Daniel dared not look back. He preferred to remember the oxen as they had been— patient, steady, always moving forward.

When they moved on, he had only four oxen to drive, though it looked as if poor old Marigold would soon give out, too. "Hold on, Marigold," he begged. "Hold on!"

That afternoon Captain Monroe advised them to suck on the smooth gray pebbles they found on the desert floor.

"What for?" Daniel asked.

"They help make spit so you won't dry out," the captain explained. "Let 'em cool off first in your pockets."

Daniel rolled his eyes at Suzannah. But when they put the pebbles in their mouths, they learned that the captain was right.

Wolves tracked them now, even by daylight. At night, Daniel helped set sagebrush fires around the edges of the wagon circle to keep them away. *God, I ask for Thy angels to surround and protect us,* he prayed. As he lay under the wagon, trying to sleep, he was glad to have the company of Lad and Lass curled at his feet. He couldn't see angels, but he could see the dogs when the howls of the wolves filled the night.

On the third morning, someone let out a blood-curdling scream. Daniel rolled out of bed and into the wagon circle, instantly awake. Shivers ran down his spine.

"What's wrong?" whispered Suzannah when she joined him outside the wagon.

Daniel shrugged, but after a while, word came up the line. "It was Garth. He says Indians are after us."

When Captain Monroe rode by, Daniel asked, "What's that about Indians?"

"It's Garth's imagination," the captain explained. "Folks sometimes go a little crazy in the desert."

Garth a little crazy? In the blinding sunshine, it made sense. His mother killed by a drunken Indian . . . all the Indians they'd seen . . . and now this heat. If only Garth could stop hating all Indians because of the action of one.

Just after noon, Mordechai rode back, covered with white dust. "The Green River!" he shouted for all to hear. "Just below them bluffs. There's good water and pine forests. We've almost made it!"

"Thank the Lord!" Daniel said. He looked at his half-dead oxen and hoped they'd make it that far.

Before long, though, the oxen smelled water and began to run with the last of their strength. "Whoa, boys!" he yelled. "Whoa!" But he couldn't stop them. They ran to the river's edge and drank until he was afraid they would burst. Nearby, Lad and Lass drank deeply, too, then plunged into the cool water.

Finally the oxen had their fill. Once the wagons were circled up facing the river and the livestock were grazing along the bank, Father told the boys to take a rest.

Peeling off his shirt, Daniel called out to Ned, "How about a swim? Come on! I'll show you how."

Ned splashed in behind him, dousing his head with the cool water. Then, seeing Lad and Lass swimming about, barking with excitement, Ned said, "If *dogs* can do it, maybe I can, too."

"For starters," Daniel said, coming up beside him, "just watch Lad and Lass and do what they do. Push off, then pull your arms back through the water like this, and kick your legs."

It took some doing, but after a while Ned was able to swim a few strokes. Garth, sitting alone, watched them from the riverbank.

"Want to swim with us?" Daniel asked when he returned to the bank.

Garth eyed him coldly. "Already been swimmin'."

"I should have asked you sooner," Daniel apologized, but Garth only glared.

His stepcousin hadn't made a single friend on the wagon train, Daniel reflected. In fact, Garth had gone out of his way to stay by himself. Instead of joining in at evening campfires, he'd take guard duty. *A loner,* Father had called him sadly.

"Sure you don't want to join us?" Daniel asked. But his stepcousin turned and headed in the opposite direction.

Daniel felt a little guilty. He hadn't tried very hard to make friends with Garth. Now he watched his stepcousin walk away, wondering if it was too late.

When he turned again to the bank, his spirits lifted. Charles had taken little Jamie into the river to play, and Pauline was sitting nearby, dangling her feet in the water. They looked like a real family for a change.

Ned had noticed Daniel's quiet mood and spoke up. "Maybe Charles and Garth can change like me . . . you know . . . since I gave my heart to Christ—"

"I hope so," Daniel said. 'But not everyone gives his heart to Christ. In fact, lots of people never do. I guess it's because they just don't understand that it's really an exciting adventure."

After the awful trek through the desert, the mountain trail ahead was what Mother and Aunt Pearl called "a blessed relief." The week's travel through high ridges and pine forests lifted their spirits, but Mordechai warned, "We're comin' to Bannock Injun country. They ain't friendly."

Daniel saw Garth's eyes narrow. *Lord, don't let there be any trouble,* Daniel prayed.

At Bear River, the trail swung northward, and the oxen seemed stronger after their rest and good food. The going was easier, too, except in a few places where canyons forced the travelers to follow the hills. After some days, though, the land again seemed endlessly dull.

Suddenly Suzannah called out, "Look ahead! It's the beginning of the soda springs!"

Daniel brightened and hurried the oxen forward. He could scarcely believe his eyes! Mordechai had spoken of springs, but not that this place would be a vast wonderland where water gushed from the earth like giant fountains.

Soda Springs shot plumes of water a hundred feet into the air; another, Steamboat Spring, rumbled like a steamboat and spewed out even taller columns. Everyone marveled as they came to one spring after another, and for supper, the women used the soda water to make biscuits and bread with what little flour remained.

That night they camped near Steamboat Spring, watching the fountains rise higher and higher in the moonlight. After the trek through the dry and barren desert, the refreshing sound of water was a delight. The journey hadn't been easy, Daniel thought as he drifted off to sleep, but they'd sure seen lots of interesting sights.

After the excitement of the springs, it was a dull ten-day pull toward Fort Hall. Daniel couldn't help thinking of

Charles's gambling, though. "Let's hope it doesn't turn out like Fort Laramie."

Riding by at that moment, his father stopped to tell them, "At Fort Hall, we'll be halfway to California."

"Only halfway?!" Daniel exclaimed.

His father nodded. "Two months further to California and four to Oregon."

How will we ever make it? Daniel wondered.

As Fort Hall came into view that afternoon, Daniel saw it was only another walled fur trading post, smaller than Fort Laramie. Fortunately, at this one, there were no tepees or Indians to be seen.

"We'll take a day's rest, repair wagons, and buy supplies here," said Captain Monroe on a swing by their wagon. "There's plenty of grass for the livestock."

It sounded fine, Daniel thought, but he felt uneasy, maybe because of Charles's gambling.

Later, as they pulled even with the white-washed walls of the fort, two men ran out. "Gold!" they shouted. "A big gold strike in California! Nuggets as big as potatoes! We're lookin' for men to ride there with us."

"First I've heard of it," said Mordechai.

One of the men produced a folded newspaper article from his shirt pocket. "Just read for yourself."

The emigrants passed the paper around with growing excitement, and Daniel read from San Francisco's *Californian* of May 29, 1848: "The whole country from San Francisco to Los Angeles to the seashore to the base of the Sierra Nevada resounds to the sordid cry of gold, gold!, GOLD! while the field is left half planted, the house half built and everything neglected but the manufacture of shovels and pick-axes."

"It's by the American River," said another. "We're going tomorrow morning. We aim to be rich!"

"Gold in California . . . gold in California!"

Word of the strike traveled around the wagon train in no time as they formed their circle. Remembering the look on Charles's face when he'd first heard the news, Daniel noticed that Charles, joined by Uncle Karl, had gone over to speak with the men again.

Daniel unyoked the oxen and led them out to graze. As he headed for the crowd by the gate of the fort, he overheard Charles say, "I'll ride on to California with you."

Pauline had caught up with Charles, and at his announcement, her face turned white. "But, Charles . . . what about me . . . and Jamie?"

"You'll be all right," Charles said, dismissing her question with a wave of his hand. "There's a fortune to be made, and you'd hold me back."

Pauline's mouth fell open, and Daniel's mother and Aunt Pearl gasped. "Sounds like Charles all right," Suzannah whispered. "Never thinks about anyone except himself."

Seeing their shock, Charles went on, "You can come along later with the wagon train to California . . . or I can meet you in Oregon after I've made our fortune."

"Might be a good idea at that," said Uncle Karl. "Some of us men could ride on ahead—"

"Why, Karl!" Aunt Pearl protested. "Surely you wouldn't leave me already!"

Others joined the discussion, and before long, some of the emigrants bound for Oregon had decided to go to California instead. "We'd get there two months sooner," they argued, "and we could always go north to Oregon later, like Charles Herrington says."

Daniel turned to his father. "What about us?"

"Yes," Mother added, "what about us?"

Daniel's father drew a deep breath. "I think we must pray very seriously about the matter. We don't want our family broken up."

"But we planned to go to Oregon," Daniel objected. "You've dreamed about going ever since you met Meriwether Lewis—"

"We'll pray about it," Father insisted. "We don't have to decide for a few days, not until we get to the Raft River. God will give us the answer when the time comes."

When the time comes, Daniel thought. He headed to the wagon. Probably God would give him the answer about his being a minister when the time came, too. Still, he couldn't believe Father would consider going to California. Not Father. Not Franklin *Meriwether* Colton.

The next morning, Charles and two of the unmarried men rode off for California with the gold seekers from Fort Hall. "See you in California in two months!" they called back over their shoulders.

Pauline wept and Suzannah muttered to Daniel, "It's not easy for me to love Charles Herrington."

"I know. He's as hard-hearted as a rock."

"Think your father will decide to go to California?" Suzannah asked.

Daniel shrugged. "Don't know. He was so set on Oregon . . . but now I'm not so sure myself."

Her eyes widened. "Why, Daniel Meriwether Colton! Don't tell me *you're* getting gold fever!"

"Not really," he replied, "but it *would* be interesting."

"You mean you want to go to California?"

He shook his head. "I don't know. It's not easy to

change direction when we've thought about nothing but Oregon for so long."

As the wagon train rattled away from Fort Hall, Daniel struggled with the question: Oregon or California? California or Oregon? With the oxen and the people so tired, maybe it would be best to go to California, then Oregon later. On the other hand, maybe they'd never get to Oregon. That night as he slept under the wagon, the question echoed in his dreams: *Oregon or California? California or Oregon?*

The wagon train moved westward along the bank of the Snake River, where the water flowed through dark lava toward Oregon. Even while he marveled at the magnificent American Falls tumbling over the rocks, his mind was busy with their decision: *Oregon or California?* There was no time to waste, either, for overhead, large flocks of geese were already flying south. Winter could still catch them in the mountains.

The second evening when they made camp, Garth headed out to hunt alone, though they had been warned against it.

"Garth!" Daniel called to him, but his stepcousin couldn't hear him.

Seeing his father and Uncle Karl helping with some wagon repairs, Daniel grabbed his rifle and headed out in the direction he had last seen Garth. Someone had to stop him.

When Daniel caught a glimpse of him hurrying through the forest, he called again, "Garth! We're not supposed to hunt alone in Bannock country!" But Garth still didn't answer. *I'm going to get myself an Indian*, he had said. Daniel's blood ran cold. Maybe this was what his stepcousin had on his mind right now!

Garth had left a careless trail of broken brush and crushed ferns; it was easy enough to follow, even for a

greenhorn. Daniel decided not to call out again. His stepcousin would be even more furious if rabbits or deer were scared off.

The woods grew thicker and the trail became less obvious. Was Garth stalking an animal? Daniel wondered. He moved quietly alongside a small stream, hoping they could find their way back to the wagons later. He should have told Father or someone—

Quite suddenly, he saw Garth in front of him, his rifle pointed at something across the stream. Daniel's eyes followed the direction in which his stepcousin was aiming his gun, expecting to see a deer or a rabbit. Instead, he saw an Indian . . . crouched low on the opposite side!

Garth stood perfectly still, sighting along the barrel into the dimness of the forest.

Daniel froze, almost afraid to move lest he startle Garth and the gun go off. Still, he had to do something!

Something inside him urged him forward. Quietly he crept just behind Garth. Then, drawing on all his strength, he threw himself at Garth.

The gunshot echoed through the forest. Garth and Daniel tumbled over the riverbank. For a long, terrible moment, Daniel didn't know whether he had come in time.

"Get off me!" Garth swore, thrashing beneath Daniel.

Looking up, Daniel spotted the Indian, poised to run. This was no Indian warrior. It was an Indian girl! The basket of berries she had been gathering lay where she had dropped it. Her black eyes, wide with fright, met his, and she turned and fled deep into the woods.

Daniel rolled off Garth's back, and the boy got up swinging. The first punch caught Daniel in the arm and almost sent him into the river. Daniel stood his ground, blocking and ducking Garth's punches, but giving none in return. "Fight, you sissy, fight!" Garth cried, swinging more and more wildly.

"That was just a *girl*," Daniel gasped, ducking again. "You almost killed a girl!"

Garth's face turned red with rage. "But they killed my ma! They killed her, and she's never comin' back!" Suddenly he stopped swinging. Angry tears filled his eyes.

Daniel backed off warily and picked up Garth's rifle. "Killing Indians won't bring her back. Your fight isn't with them. It's with the devil. Don't you see? Only Christ can help you—"

"Git out of there!" Both boys looked up to see a figure in deerskin standing above them on the riverbank. It was Mordechai!

"Git out of there afore the whole Bannock tribe comes down on us," he said. "I been trailing you. Now git!"

Quickly the boys scrambled up the bank and followed Mordechai through the forest, stopping here and there to listen for footsteps behind them. There was nothing except the sounds of small woodland creatures and the sigh of the breeze through the trees.

Reaching the edge of the woods, Mordechai halted and gripped Garth's arm. His voice was stern. "If Dan'l hadn't put his life on the line, boy, you'd a got us all kilt."

Garth dropped his head, unable to look either of them in the eye. "Yes, sir," he mumbled.

"Here." Daniel offered Garth's rifle to him. Surprised, Garth took it. Daniel gave him a long look. "I won't tell, Garth. It'll be between us. Right, Mordechai?"

The old man nodded solemnly.

Without another word, Garth took off running. Mordechai and Daniel watched him until he was out of sight. Then they walked together to the campsite.

After a while the old guide spoke. "When I first saw you, Dan'l, I figgered you had the mark of a real man about you. Today I seen it agin."

"I'm still no frontiersman," Daniel objected.

"You're larnin', son, you're larnin'. Besides, frontier-in' ain't near as important as bein' godly. That's what Bible-totin' Jedediah Smith told me hisself."

Daniel's heart filled with hope. "He did?"

"Thet he did," Mordechai replied, his wispy white beard blowing in the early evening breeze. "Thet he did."

EPILOGUE

That night they doubled the guard. But the Indians didn't come. Daniel decided it was because the Indian girl hadn't told them about the shooting. Or maybe she'd explained that a white boy had saved her life. Either way, she was safe, and they were, too . . . for now anyway. Even the question of whether to go to California or Oregon no longer seemed as important. Far more important was listening to that still, small voice of the Lord.

The next day, the Raft River came into view. Now was the time to make the decision: California or Oregon.

Just before dinner, the family gathered around the table for prayer. When they joined hands, Garth actually let Aunt Pearl take his hand. Daniel smiled quickly at them, then ducked his head.

"Lord, guide us clearly in the decision we must make tonight," Father prayed. "Will it be California or Oregon? Where would Thou have us go? We shall now listen in silence for Thy leading."

Daniel listened over the twitter of birds by the river, half-hoping to hear a great voice from heaven booming out: "California!" or even "Oregon!" so they'd be certain. Instead, it was the same small voice he had come to recognize: *Hold the family together. Hold the family together. . . .* The words hung in the air for a long time, and Daniel felt a great peace inside.

At last, Father ended the prayer. "We thank Thee, Lord. Amen."

They all turned to him, and Father's sun-browned face broke into a wide Colton grin. "We're going to the California Territory for now. I believe God wants us to join Charles, to hold the family together."

Just what God had told him! Daniel thought.

Suzannah grinned at Daniel, and he grinned back. All of a sudden he felt a most ungodly urge to yank one of her braids, so he did. Then he yanked it again.

"Daniel Meriwether Colton!" Suzannah fumed.

Before she could strike back, he was racing toward the river. "California, here we come!" he yelled.

"But not before I get you!" she called, and took off after him.

Go West With
Suzannah and Daniel Colton!

Suzannah and the Secret Coins

When twelve-year-old Suzannah Colton is told to pack up her things to move West, the adventure has only just begun. On the National Road from Alexandria, Virginia to Independence, Missouri, she encounters bears, blizzards, and other dangers. But can she keep her secret coins hidden from her wicked brother-in-law, Charles?

Daniel Colton Under Fire

Daniel Colton has just turned thirteen, and he's out to prove himself a man. But he's grown up in the city. Does he have what it takes to make it in the Wild West? A hunting accident, a near-drowning, and other wild adventures on the Oregon Trail test the limits of Daniel's courage.

Suzannah Strikes Gold

When the Coltons arrive in California in the midst of the Gold Rush, Suzannah catches gold fever. But instead of helping the family, the gold she finds plunges the family into even more trouble.

Daniel Colton Kidnapped

Life seems to return to normal when the Colton family buys a house near San Francisco. Then Daniel's father opens a most unusual store, and Charles begins to pressure Daniel to work for him secretly. Can Daniel untangle himself from the web of evil and deceit that threatens the whole family?

*Look for the Colton Cousins Adventures
at your local Christian bookstore.*